The House on the Corner

The House on the Corner

Some houses are ahead of their time

Dan Curtis

Dan Curtis
Visit my website at https://dancurtismusic.com

Printed in the United States of America

ISBN: 979-8-9894479-0-9

PROLOGUE

The large, beautiful Victorian house that George Holman built in 1920 didn't fit well into the rural American countryside. Such an ostentatious home in a simple rural community caused no small stir among his neighbors.

Some of the townsfolk reasoned that he built the house to remind himself of his English upbringing. Others conjectured that he wanted to flaunt his wealth and establish himself as a prominent member of the community. But George never associated much with his neighbors. He mostly kept to himself.

While the townspeople ruminated and gossiped about the new European family in their midst, some of the more level-headed citizens suggested that George was just following the time-honored tradition of family and generation homes, in which the home was intended to be passed down through generations, serving as a family estate and a place for future family members to live. Indeed, that was part of George's plan, but it was secondary to the real reason he built the house.

The house was ahead of its time in many ways – some of them visible, some of them not. In keeping with classic Victorian architecture, the house had bay windows and cylindrical turrets, complete with spires. But the spacious home also possessed a subtle futuristic atmosphere. It was the first home in the countryside to have electricity and indoor plumbing. It had a telephone. Indeed, it seemed to be a house of the future, which provided a hint about the reason for its existence.

George Holman's house had nothing to do with affluence, tradition or nostalgia. He was hiding something he didn't want anybody to know about. His house was built to hide a device that could alter the past and future and he was determined to keep it safe and out of the hands of people who would use it for malevolent purposes.

Chapter One

1920 – A House Is Built at the Edge of Town

George Holman kept looking over his shoulder as he, his wife, and two children disembarked the ship at New York Harbor. The journey across the Atlantic had taken nearly a week and George had been on edge the whole time, worried that somebody was following them. Maybe it was just his nervous nature.

He and his family had been living in the Netherlands and boarded a ship in the port of Amsterdam for America. His wife, Greta, was German, and after the Great War, German expatriates had experienced a new level of prejudice and hostility. George and Greta hoped to settle down in a small town in rural America and escape the problems they had faced because of Greta's German heritage.

The family had traveled first class, so they had received an immigration inspection aboard the ship, which enabled them to skip the long lines that third class passengers would have to wait in at Ellis Island. Third class passengers generally traveled in crowded conditions at the bottom of steamships, where they were subjected to dirty conditions and disease. When the ship docked at New York Harbor, they were herded onto a ferry and transported to Ellis Island for detailed inspections, which included medical exams by doctors, looking for coughs, wheezing and a host of diseases. Doctors would even make mothers put down their children to make sure they could walk and didn't have polio or other diseases.

These exams resulted in sick people being sent to hospital wards on Ellis Island. Families were often separated and sometimes returned to their homeland because of illnesses that authorities didn't want to come into the United States. But the medical exams were not what worried George. He was concerned about his German wife, Greta. How would she be treated in their new home? And more immediately, by the immigration official aboard the ship.

During their immigration inspection, the official had only glanced at George's British documentation before stamping it and handing it back to him. But when he looked at Greta's documentation and saw that she was German, his pleasant demeanor immediately changed, and his smile turned to a frown.

"So, you're German, Mrs. Holman?" the inspector inquired in an accusing tone.

"Yes," Greta answered quietly. She was obviously nervous and worried about what might happen if the inspector was prejudiced against Germans.

"How did you folks meet?" the official pried.

George was quick to answer. "I was working as a press correspondent in the Netherlands before the war broke out. I met my wife there."

"I see," the official said smugly. "And you have two children?"

"Yes," George answered. "This is Josef," he said, pointing to the older child. "He's thirteen years old. And this is Annie," he said, touching his daughter's shoulder. "She's ten."

The official looked at the children for a few moments before continuing. "And what will you do in America?" he asked.

"We hope to start a new life," George answered. "Europe has been torn apart by war. America offers hope of a life we can never have anywhere else."

His answer seemed to be acceptable to the official, who handed Greta's papers back and said, "Welcome to America, Mr. and Mrs. Holman."

The family made their way to the train station that would take them west to their ultimate destination: a rural community in the Midwest.

Greta took the children and boarded the train while George personally oversaw the transfer of their luggage from the ship to the train. Once their luggage was secured aboard the train the family began the second leg of their journey by land. George began to feel a little more at ease as they settled into their compartment. Their destination was not chosen by chance. George had been planning the move carefully and had researched viable locations in America where the family could start a new life and leave the old world behind them.

The small family of four arrived in town in the spring of 1920. The European couple stood out from the other folks in the rural American town. George spoke with a British accent, and Greta had a thick German accent. Despite her heavy accent, her English was very good. The new immigrants instantly became the subject of gossip.

Soon after their arrival, George bought a piece of land on the edge of town. He paid cash, which raised eyebrows among the locals and added to their gossip and speculation about the couple. George and Greta pitched a couple of tents and set up camp on one end of the property. The family lived in one tent and their belongings were carefully stored in the other tent. Greta and Annie busied themselves with domestic chores while George and Josef went to work building a house.

The Holman's seemed to have plenty of money at their disposal. Occasionally, George would come to town and send a wire to a bank in Switzerland. Soon, money would arrive through Western Union. He used the money to buy supplies and materials for his house. The Holman's were an enigma. Except for brief encounters, they were a complete mystery to the townspeople and that's the way George wanted to keep it; at least until he finished his house.

Over the next couple of years, the Holman family kept to themselves and rarely left their property except for supplies. The community watched from afar as the house was built. Helpful neighbors sometimes showed up with tools in hand and offered to help, but they were politely turned away. George seemed to have plenty of help, but snoopy neighbors did not recognize any of the workers. It seemed that George had brought people in from outside the community to help build his house, but nobody ever saw them arrive or leave.

The project started with a basement. George, his young son and their mysterious helpers worked from sunup to sundown digging the hole. Once the basement was done, the outside walls went up quickly.

When the walls, doors and windows were up George and Greta dismantled their camp and moved their family into the house. Even though it wasn't finished, it was certainly more comfortable than the tents they had been living in.

The furniture was selected from local stores. The furnishings were delivered and placed throughout the new home. The delivery crews were amazed by the interior of the home. It had electricity and indoor plumbing, which was extremely rare, especially in rural areas. The lavish interior of the home matched the sleek exterior and added to the gossip about town.

Soon, shipments of large crates began arriving at the Holman's new home. The crates were left at the front of the house for George to open and unload. He always opened them in the dark of night and moved the contents into the house when it was hard for people to see. The neighbors were naturally curious about the mysterious crates that kept coming to the house, but nobody was able to get close enough to find out what they contained. Once the crates were unloaded, they were broken apart and burned.

Over time, visible activity at the house died down but rumors and gossip persisted. The most prevalent rumor was that the Holmans were bank robbers and had come to the small, rural town to hide from authorities. The outsiders who helped them with their house were suspected to be accomplices.

Another rumor was that George had been a soldier in the British army during the Great War and had plundered precious artworks and antiques and had them shipped to their new home in the United States. According to town gossip, some of the plunder had probably been sold and the money deposited into a Swiss bank account.

Once they were settled into their new home, George and Greta decided it was time to let down their guard and get to know their neighbors. Fred and Harriet Johnson had two boys that were close in age to Josef and Annie. The Johnsons accepted a dinner invitation and came over on a Thursday afternoon with their children. Josef and Annie took the Johnson boys upstairs to play in their rooms while the adults visited in the kitchen. Greta was busy preparing dinner when she realized that she needed some things to complete the meal. She called up to Annie to come downstairs.

"I need you to go down to the basement and get some cabbage and potatoes." Greta said when her daughter came into the kitchen.

Annie simply nodded her head and disappeared around the corner to the hallway as the adults continued their conversation. Moments later, they heard Annie scream. They rushed down to the basement and found the young girl huddled up against the wall at the base of the stairs.

"What's wrong?" George asked as he came to the bottom of the stairs.

Annie pointed to the other side of the room. He turned and looked in the direction she was pointing and saw a man lying on the floor. Greta took Annie in her arms as George cautiously crossed the room to examine the body. Thinking that it might be a sleeping hobo he nudged the man with his foot. The body was stiff and cold. The man had no pulse.

"He's dead," George announced, turning around to talk to Greta and the Johnsons, who were standing at the base of the stairs.

"Take Annie upstairs," George said to Greta. "Mr. Johnson, would you please dial the sheriff?"

"With a telephone?" Fred stammered.

"Yes, there's one in the parlor upstairs."

"I don't know how to use it."

"Just pick up the handpiece and tell the operator you need to be connected with the police."

The Johnsons bounded up the stairs, anxious to get away from the dead body. Fred located the telephone and stared at it momentarily before picking up the earpiece and raising it to his ear. Soon, he heard a voice through the receiver. "Operator, how may I connect your call?"

"Uh," he stammered. "This is Fred Johnson. There's a dead man at the Holman's new house."

"I'll connect you with the sheriff," the voice on the other end said.

Fred relayed the same information to a deputy before placing the earpiece back on the phone.

The sheriff soon arrived with a deputy and banged on the door. "What's all this about a dead body?" the sheriff demanded as Greta opened the door.

"Down in the basement," Fred Johnson said, pointing to the stairs. The men trudged down the steps and found George in the basement with the body.

"What's the trouble?" the sheriff demanded gruffly.

"My daughter came down here to get some potatoes and found this gentleman laying here," George explained. "At first, I thought it was a hobo, but there are no belongings down here with him. I have no idea how he got down here."

The deputy ushered everybody upstairs to the living room and took statements from George, Greta, and the Johnsons. Nobody had any knowledge or information about the dead man. The medical examiner came, and the deputy escorted him downstairs to examine the body. He came back upstairs about 15 minutes later and asked to use the phone to call for a crew to come pick up the corpse.

While they waited for the ambulance to arrive, the medical examiner shared his preliminary findings. "The man downstairs was killed by blunt force trauma to the head," he explained. "There isn't any blood because the skin was not broken by the blow."

The sheriff also shared his observations. "It looks like the victim was killed right where he is laying. The floor downstairs is a little dusty and there's no evidence that the body was dragged down there."

"Are you saying the man was murdered in our house?" George asked.

"Yes," the sheriff replied. "Which means that somebody in this house probably killed him."

"I beg to differ, Sheriff," George objected. "I can't explain how that man got down there, but nobody in this house killed him, I assure you."

"Well, Mr. Holman," the sheriff said with a slight hint of irritation. "There's a dead man in your basement. And you claim that you don't know how he got into the house. But he was either an invited guest or snuck in somehow. The fact remains that he's dead and he's in your house. It's highly unlikely that somebody killed him and dumped him in your basement, so the logical conclusion is that somebody in this house killed him. Now, do you want to tell me what really happened here?"

Two men arrived in an ambulance with a gurney. The deputy led them down to the basement. Suddenly, the deputy was heard yelling for someone to stop. The sounds of a scuffle prompted the sheriff to race to the basement followed by George and the coroner. The three men arrived at the bottom of the stairs just in time to see somebody crawling out through the basement window. The deputy was trying to drag him back inside but lost his grip and the man disappeared into the night.

"What happened?" The sheriff demanded.

"When we got down here," the deputy panted, "We found a man trying to climb out the window. I tried grabbing him but, he got away."

The sheriff and the deputy pounded back up the stairs and rushed outside to apprehend the man. They searched the area with flashlights to no avail. They gave up the search and went back to the basement to deal with the corpse. They found the ambulance crew and George in the basement, but the body was gone.

"Where's the body?" the sheriff demanded.

The two men by the gurney shook their heads and shrugged. "There wasn't a body down here when we got here, just the man trying to escape out the window."

"Perhaps I was in error," George replied. "Maybe the man wasn't dead after all. My guess is that he woke up and escaped through the window."

"I examined that body," the coroner said with a hint of irritation in his voice. "He was dead all right."

"Then how do you account for the fact that the body is gone?" George inquired.

The coroner didn't have an answer.

"I don't know what's going on here, but this is the strangest thing I've ever seen," the sheriff exclaimed.

"I think the situation is quite straightforward," George replied. "Clearly, a man snuck into my basement and hit his head. In all the excitement, we all rushed to judgement that the man was dead, when, obviously, he was just knocked unconscious. When he woke up, he escaped out the window and ran."

The coroner shook his head but decided against arguing. The orderlies who came to pick up the body dragged and their gurney upstairs and left with the coroner.

George thanked the sheriff and deputy for their services and was relieved when they finally left. But nobody was happier to leave than the Johnsons. They practically ran from the house once the sheriff excused them.

Chapter Two

1922 – The Haunted House

"I think this house is haunted," nine-year-old Annie announced.

The Holman family was gathered around the dining room table, eating dinner.

"Why do you say that?" George asked his daughter.

"Remember the dead man we found in the basement a few weeks ago?" she asked.

"Yes," George answered.

"Well, I think he's haunting the house."

"That guy didn't die," fifteen-year-old Josef objected. "He woke up and climbed out the window."

"Oh, he died alright," Annie said confidently. "And now he's haunting the house."

"Why do you think someone is haunting the house?" George asked.

"Because I see a man in the house sometimes," Annie replied. "And sometimes he talks to me."

"Wow," Josef interjected. "That's creepy!"

Greta stopped eating and put down her fork.

"What does this man talk to you about?" She asked earnestly.

"He always asks me about some kind of treasure that he thinks is hidden in the basement."

"Treasure?" George asked, his brow furrowing. "What kind of treasure does he think is down there?"

"I don't know," Annie responded. "He tries to get me to play this game like he's a pirate and there's buried treasure. He asks me where he should look."

"Have you helped him look for treasure?" George asked.

"No. I told him there isn't any treasure in the basement."

"What does the man look like?" George asked.

"He has dark hair and a beard."

"How do you know he's a ghost?" Josef asked. "How do you know he's not some psycho?"

"Because he can disappear."

"Really?" George asked. "How does he disappear?"

"Well," Annie began. "It always happens in the basement. Sometimes when I'm down there, he just appears and starts talking to me. Then he just disappears."

George and Greta looked at each other with concern in their eyes.

"Next time the ghost appears, can you come get me?" George asked. "I'd like to meet him."

"Okay Daddy," Annie agreed.

"How about you, Josef?" George asked. "Have you seen this ghost?"

"No," Josef replied. "But I have heard voices in the house. It's kind of eerie. Oh, and I have seen a guy walking around on our property. And the weird thing is, he looks a lot like the guy Annie described."

"Why haven't you said anything about this man?" George inquired. "He could be the man that broke into our house."

"I don't know. I didn't think it was a big deal," Josef answered. "And as for the voices at night; I just thought I was hearing things."

The conversation turned to school and homework. Annie was in seventh grade and Josef was a sophomore in high school. Josef was a lackluster student, but Annie loved school. She had a lot of school friends. Josef on the other hand was a bit of a loner. Aside from a few close friends, he didn't associate much with other students.

Lately, Josef had been hearing rumors going around the school about his family, so he brought the subject up during dinner. "What do you do for a living, Dad?" Josef asked.

"I'm retired," George answered. "Why do you ask?"

"Kids at school are saying that you were a bank robber and that you hid a bunch of money here at the house."

George chuckled. "Are they really?"

"Yeah," Josef said. "Is it true?"

"Heaven's no," George answered. "I've never robbed a bank in my life."

"So where does our money come from?" Josef persisted.

George glanced at his wife before answering the question. He paused while he gathered his thoughts, making sure he framed the answer appropriately.

"Both your mother and I come from families that had money. Most of our money came from inheritances. Then we invested it to create more money and that's what we live on."

"Oh," Josef said, sheepishly. "I didn't know."

"Don't pay any attention to rumors, Josef," George said. "People make things up when they don't understand something."

Later that night, George and Greta discussed the conversation they'd had with their children during dinner as they got ready for bed.

"Are you concerned about this ghost Annie was talking about?" Greta asked in her German accent.

"I don't know," George replied. "I don't believe in ghosts. Maybe she's making it up, like an imaginary friend."

"But what if it's a real person? What if they're after our possessions?"

"Well, I thought that might be what it was at first until she said that the man or ghost disappeared. That's what makes me think that it's an imaginary friend."

"But Josef said he's seen a man outside like the one Annie described," Greta argued.

"Yes," George agreed. "That is concerning. We'll have to keep an eye out."

George and Greta climbed into bed, turned out the light and drifted off to sleep. At 1:00 am, they were suddenly awakened by a crashing sound downstairs. They both sat straight up in bed.

"What was that?" Greta asked, her heart racing from the sudden interruption of her sleep.

"I don't know," George answered. "Listen, I think I hear voices. It sounds like somebody is arguing downstairs."

The couple strained to hear what sounded like a heated argument between two men somewhere downstairs. Or maybe outside. It was hard to pinpoint the location of the sound.

"Someone is in our house," Greta gasped, clutching her husband's arm.

George jumped out of bed and raced to the closet. He grabbed a double barrel shotgun and some shells then headed toward the bedroom door.

"George, what are you doing? Shouldn't we call the police?" Greta implored.

"The phone is downstairs, darling. We must go down there anyway so why not take some protection?"

George walked through the door and into the hallway. Then he poked his head back into the room. "You stay here," he told Greta. "I'll check things out."

"Be careful," she responded.

George creeped into the second-floor hallway and switched on the light. With a firm grip on his gun, he cautiously walked down the stairs to the first floor. As he reached the bottom and turned on the light, he heard Annie's voice at the top of the stairs behind him.

"What's happening, Daddy?" she asked, innocently. "I heard a loud noise that woke me up."

"It's okay, sweetie," George said. "Go back to bed."

Josef appeared beside Annie, rubbing his eyes. "What's going on, Dad? What was that noise?"

"I don't know," George answered. "But I want both of you to go back to your rooms and close the door."

"Why do you have a gun, Daddy?" Annie asked.

"Just to be safe, Annie," George said, trying to sooth her anxiety. "Now please go back to your rooms. I'll find out what's going on but I'm sure everything is okay."

Josef and Annie nodded their heads, then turned and walked back down the hallway to their rooms. When George heard their doors close, he continued his search for the sounds that woke them all up. But just as suddenly as they started, the noises and angry voices ceased. George walked through all the rooms on the first floor. Everything was okay. Nothing had been disturbed. Finding nothing amiss he almost found himself beginning to believe in ghosts. Then he realized that he hadn't checked the basement. His heart began beating fast. What if there was another dead body down there? It was better that he found it than his young daughter.

He threw open the basement door and aimed his shotgun down the stairs only to find that it was dark. He couldn't see more than a few feet ahead. He quickly smacked the light switch and breathed a sigh of relief when the light revealed an empty stairwell. He quietly tiptoed down the steps, half expecting someone, or something to jump out at him when he reached the bottom. Nothing did.

He switched on the light in the basement and aimed his gun as he looked around the room. It appeared that nothing had been disturbed here as well. But then he looked at the floor. It was covered in blood. Not puddles of blood, but a lot of blood, nonetheless. It seemed to coat the floor in streaks as though there had been a bloody brawl and somebody had been dragged through it.

George wasted no time bounding up the stairs. He dialed the sheriff as fast as his fingers could navigate the rotary dial phone in the parlor. It seemed an eternity while the shaken family waited for the authorities to arrive. Greta and the children had come downstairs and were waiting in the living room. George kept a tight grip on the shotgun, ready to shoot anything that moved. Luckily, nothing did.

Finally, a deputy arrived. George told him about the noises that woke the family up and the angry voices they heard and how George grabbed his shotgun and went downstairs, ultimately finding blood on the basement floor.

"Well, let's go down and take a look," the deputy said when the family finished telling their individual versions of the story.

George picked up his shotgun and was headed toward the basement door when the deputy stopped him.

"Sir, would you mind leaving the shotgun up here?" the deputy asked. "I've got my service revolver, so I think we're safe. Besides, you're making me nervous with that thing."

George agreed and set the gun down before leading the deputy down to the basement. He began to point out the blood on the floor, but it was gone. The floor was clean.

"I swear, the last time I came down here there was blood all over the floor," George said in embarrassment.

The deputy looked around the floor then cocked his head at George. "Isn't this where ya'll found a dead body a while back that then disappeared?"

"Yes," George admitted. "Yes, it is."

"Well, I don't know what to tell ya, Mr. Holman. Maybe this place is haunted."

George nodded. "At this point, deputy, I actually find that thought rather comforting."

George and the deputy went back upstairs where Greta and the children were anxiously waiting.

"No blood downstairs, folks," the deputy said. "I think you're safe for tonight, so go to bed and get some sleep."

The deputy wished the family a good night and tipped his hat as he left. George closed the front door and turned to his family who were huddled together in the entryway. He stared at his wife and kids for a moment.

"Well," he said, breaking the silence. "It appears that our house is haunted."

"What happened?" Greta asked. "How did the blood just disappear?"

"I guess it disappeared the same way that the body did. I can't explain it."

Josef and Annie were too scared to sleep in their own rooms that night, so they slept on the floor in George and Greta's room. After the kids fell asleep, George and Greta discussed the events of the evening."

"Do you really think the house is haunted?" Greta asked.

"I don't know what to think," George replied. "I've never believed in ghosts but the things that have been happening surely seem supernatural." The couple's conversation waned as they drifted off to sleep.

The next morning, after Annie and Josef left for school, George went down to the basement to examine it more closely. The strange events really bothered him, and he wanted to find answers. Moreover, he wanted to make sure the house he built for his family was safe and secure.

He shined a flashlight around the room, looking for anything he might have missed in the dark of night. As he shined his light in the far corner of the room, he saw something glisten on the floor. He walked over and picked it up. It appeared to be a broken piece of a bottle and it was covered in dried blood. He looked over to the other side of the room where he kept a small wine rack. One of his prized bottles of red wine was missing.

George admittedly didn't know much about ghosts, but he was pretty sure they were not corporeal. The shard of glass he found proved that somebody or something had been in the basement that night. And whatever or whoever they were, they had been fighting, and broke one of his bottles of wine in the process. He suspected that he had interrupted their fight and they fled, then one of them came back to clean up the mess before the deputy arrived. But what concerned him the most was the possibility that they had discovered his secret.

Chapter Three

Present Day - Tragedy

The house that George Holman built at the edge of town in 1920 was eventually incorporated into the town proper as the community grew and spread beyond the old house. Over time, a neighborhood sprang up around it and the house occupied a prominent position on the corner of the entrance to the neighborhood.

It didn't blend well with the other houses in the area. It was a large, two-story Victorian house with a large attic, bay windows and a wraparound porch. It had a steep imposing roofline with a fireplace that rose high into the sky. Cylindrical turrets with spires rose above the roofline and added to the asymmetrical layout of the house.

The house had been in the family for generations when it became the home of Thomas and Janet Holman. Thomas and his younger brother, Jake, had grown up in the house. Jake and his wife, Mia, now lived a few blocks away.

Thomas was seven years older than Jake. The brothers were nothing alike. Thomas was an accountant and liked things to be orderly and consistent. He was perfectly happy living a predictable and uneventful life. Jake often teased him about this aspect of his character, telling him that he lived his life by generally accepted accounting principles.

Jake was a contractor. He loved sports and outdoor activities. He had a gym membership and worked out often. He drove a big truck and loved driving it through the mud after a rain. Thomas on the other hand lived his life in a chair. He got very little exercise, and his physique showed it. He drove a Volvo; not because it was prestigious, but because he thought it was a safe vehicle.

Jake spoke with a masculine, confident voice. Thomas' voice was a little higher pitched and a bit nerdy. If he sang, he would be a tenor, but he couldn't sing on key to save his life.

On a warm, balmy summer evening Thomas had invited Jake and Mia over for a barbeque. The brothers were outside by the grill. Thomas was busy cooking while Jake relaxed in a lawn chair. Having grown up in the house, the brothers had heard all the ghost stories that supposedly happened there, which was the subject of their current conversation.

"There's some really creepy stuff going on in this house, Jake!" Thomas said as he flipped the burgers over on the grill.

"You know, we're all grown up now, Thomas," Jake replied. "I think we can put away the old ghost stories. They were fun when we were kids, but -"

"No, Dude, this place is really haunted," Thomas insisted.

"Okay," Jake replied, trying to humor his brother. "Why do you think it's haunted?"

"Because I wake up at night, hearing someone in the house. I'll grab my baseball bat and flashlight and walk around the house, but I never find anybody there."

"So, because you never find anybody in the house you think the noises must be caused by ghosts?"

"Yeah, what else could it be?" Thomas asked.

"Well, this is an old house, Thomas. It's made of wood. We grew up in this house and I remember hearing creaks and groans when we were kids. I used to think it was haunted too, but then I grew up. The house is even older now than when we were kids, so I imagine those creaks and groans have only gotten worse."

"Yeah, but this is different, man. I swear I hear somebody talking in the house at night. Janet has heard it too."

Janet and Mia were in the kitchen having their own conversation. But it had nothing to do with ghosts. They were discussing more practical matters while they prepared dinner.

"So, are you guys planning to have kids?" Janet asked while dropping ears of corn into a pot.

Jake and Mia had been married two years but didn't have any children. They met when Jake moved back to town after a four-year stint in the Army. Mia had just graduated college with a teaching degree and was a first-year elementary school teacher.

Mia answered a little shyly, "We haven't really discussed it much, but I think we'll have kids at some point."

"Yeah, you guys have plenty of time. Thomas and I were married about three years before Tawny was born."

The two women paused their conversation as they looked out the window at the brothers and the children in the backyard.

"What do you think they're talking about?" Janet asked, motioning toward the brothers talking by the grill.

"I don't know," Mia answered. "But I doubt it has anything to do with children."

The brothers continued to reminisce about creepy memories while Thomas busied himself at the grill and his children played in the backyard.

"Remember how we used to be afraid of the basement?" Jake asked.

"I'm still afraid of the basement," Thomas answered. "I won't go down there unless I have to."

"Well, you went down there to check for ghosts, right?"

"No way," Thomas sputtered. "That's the one place I haven't checked when I've heard stuff at night. I just keep the door locked and hope nothing's down there."

"You're kidding, right?"

"No!" Thomas said emphatically. "I'm not going down there. No way!"

"When's the last time you checked out the basement, Thomas?"

"Uh, well…it's been a long time. I hate the basement, man. Too many creepy memories from childhood."

"Thomas, you have to go down there once in a while just to check on things," Jake said.

"Why?"

"Well, what if the basement floods?" Jake replied.

"Not goin' down there, Bro!"

The brothers' conversation was interrupted as a Frisbee glided past them. Jake jumped up and caught it. Thomas' 8-year-old daughter, Tawny, was trying to teach her younger brother, Jeffrey, how to catch and throw the toy.

Janet and Mia came out to the patio and laid out the buns and condiments for the meal.

"You guys ready to eat?" Janet called out.

"The burgers are coming off the grill, Sweetie," Thomas said as he scooped up the last burger and dropped it onto a plate.

Jake brought the plate of freshly cooked hamburgers to the patio table while Thomas turned off the gas to the grill. The kids dropped their Frisbee and came running to the table.

"Kids, go wash your hands before you touch the food," Janet said.

The youngsters filed into the house to comply. As Janet sat down at the table, she realized that she had left her drink in the kitchen.

"Oops," she said as she got up. "I need to get my drink. Anybody need anything from the kitchen?"

"I think we're all good," Thomas replied.

Janet returned to the backyard with drink in hand. Tawny and Jeffrey bounded past her and took their places at the patio table.

"So, what have you ladies been talking about?" Thomas asked as they all sat down at the table.

"Oh, just the usual things women talk about when their husbands aren't around," Janet said.

"Oh yeah?" Thomas asked. "What's that?"

"Girl talk is supposed to stay between girls," Mia said, pretending to be serious.

"Yeah," Thomas said. "Besides, girl talk is boring."

His comment caused a distinct moment of awkwardness. Janet, knowing her husband's clumsy social nature, deflected the conversation back to Jake and Thomas. "So, what have you guys been talking about?"

Jake brought up the conversation about ghosts just to rib his brother a bit.

"It's true," Janet said after hearing Jake tease her husband about being afraid of ghosts. "I've heard the voices too."

Jake was too pragmatic to get sucked into a conversation about ghosts.

"Well, it's an old house and old houses have a lot of creaks and groans," he argued.

"Yeah, but the noises we're hearing aren't creaks and groans," Janet replied. "Lately, we've been hearing voices and footsteps at night. Thomas and I have walked through the house every time we've heard the noises and we've never found anything out of place."

"Except," Jake continued cautiously. "You've never checked down in the basement according to Thomas."

Janet paused as she thought about it. "I never thought about it, but yeah, you're right. Why haven't we checked the basement, Thomas?" she asked turning toward him. "We've heard stuff down there too, right?"

Thomas' face suddenly went pale. Everybody stopped eating and looked at him. Tawny and Jeffrey sat with their eyes fixated on their father, waiting for his response. Jake finally broke the silence, hoping to spare his brother embarrassment, and build him up in his children's eyes.

Turning to Tawny and Jeffrey, he said, "You know, your dad used to tell me scary stories about the basement when we were kids. He had me so scared when I was little that I wouldn't go down in the basement. It is pretty creepy down there."

Tawny's eyes grew big. "What kind of stories did my dad tell you?"

Jake seemed to ignore her question. "Do you remember that, Thomas?" Jake asked.

Thomas recovered and chimed in. "Yeah, I used to tell Uncle Jake that there was a mummy in the basement. I told him if he went down there, the mummy would get him."

Jeffery was clearly bothered by this news. "Is there really a mummy down there, Daddy?" he asked, his voice trembling.

"No, of course not. I shouldn't have brought it up."

"Will you go down there and check, Daddy?" Jeffrey pleaded. "I'm scared. I don't want the mummy to get me!"

Thomas and Jake tried to reassure the kids that there was nothing down in the basement, but Jeffrey was obviously frightened and wasn't going to let the matter go unless he received an assurance that the basement was safe and secure.

Finally, Janet pleaded, "Hey, why don't you two big, strong men go down and check out the basement?"

The brothers looked at each other for a moment. Jake got up and motioned toward the door. "C'mon, Thomas. Let's go check it out."

"Now?" Thomas stammered. "Don't you want to finish your dinner first?"

"Naw," Jake replied. "It'll only take a minute or two. Let's go check it out so we can honestly tell Jeffrey that there's nothing to be afraid of."

Thomas remained in his chair, staring at Jake. His face betrayed the fear he felt inside. Jake finally broke the awkward silence.

"C'mon. A quick look downstairs and you can stop worrying about what's down there."

Thomas slowly rose from his chair and followed Jake into the house.

"Way to go," Thomas muttered to Jake as they walked. "You just had to bring up all that stuff at the dinner table..."

"Sorry, I was just making conversation. I didn't realize it would scare the kids."

"Well, it's a good thing you didn't tell them the stories Dad used to tell us about how the original owner of the house found a dead body in the basement right after they moved in."

"How is that scarier than a mummy in the basement?" Jake asked. "They're both dead people."

The basement door was locked. The door was old and still had the original lock that required a skeleton key to open it. All the other doors had been updated over the years, but the basement door still had the original lock, which somehow made the whole expedition to the basement much creepier.

Thomas pulled the old key from his pocket and inserted it into the lock. Jake noticed the ancient lock and key and took opportunity to tease Thomas about it.

"I can't believe you still have a skeleton key to this door, Thomas. That thing is ancient. Why don't you change the lock?"

"Because I never planned to go down here."

Thomas turned the key in the lock, which squeaked and clicked as the key was turned. The door creaked on its rusty hinges as it slowly swung open, revealing the dusty staircase that led to the basement. The brothers were met with cold, stale air as they toggled the light switch at the top of the stairs. The light didn't turn on. Thomas flipped the switch again but still the light didn't come on.

"Go grab another bulb," Jake said, almost whispering.

"I don't have any spare bulbs in the house," Thomas answered, thinking of how much worse the trip downstairs would be without light.

"Flashlight?" Jake asked.

"Oh, yeah. I've got one right here in the hall closet."

Thomas opened the door opposite the basement door, rummaged through the closet and pulled out a large flashlight.

"Where's your baseball bat?" Jake asked.

"It's upstairs in the bedroom. Want me to go get it?"

"No, I'm just kidding."

But Jake was only half kidding. As the brothers descended the stairs with only the dim light of the flashlight, Jake began remembering the fear he had of the basement as a child. The stories Thomas told him of mummies and goblins only heightened his childhood fears. But he wasn't going to tell Thomas. One of them, he thought, needed to act like an adult.

The stairs were covered with a layer of dust that had accumulated over the years. The brothers descended the stairs slowly, leaving footprints in the dust behind them. When they reached the bottom of the stairs, Thomas felt around for another light switch. He finally found it and flipped it, but the light didn't come on. The basement light was burned out too.

"Geez, Thomas," Jake chided. "Have you ever been down here?"

"Not since Janet and I got married and moved into the house. Dad was still alive then, remember? Mom had died and Dad lived here alone. He invited Janet and me to live here and eventually gave us the house just before he passed. We came down here once with Dad when we first moved in. He told us the story about the dead body the original owner - our great great-great-granddad, or whatever he was - found down here and even pointed out where the body was laying. He said the weird thing was that the body disappeared. After that trip down here with Dad, I locked the door and haven't opened it until tonight."

Jake tried peering into the darkness as Thomas randomly shined the light around the room.

"Maybe we should come back when I get some new light bulbs," Thomas whispered.

"No," Jake whispered back. "We're here now, so let's look around so we can honestly tell Jeffrey that there's nothing down in the basement. If you've really been hearing strange noises, we need to make sure everything's okay."

Jake pulled out his mobile phone, turned on the flashlight and shined it around the room. A few dusty books sat on a shelf on an otherwise empty bookcase. An old cabinet sat against the wall adjacent to the bookcase. Everything was covered in dust except for the cabinet.

"What's in that old cabinet?" Jake asked.

"What cabinet?" Thomas asked, looking across the room at the cabinet Jake was shining his light on. "I don't remember that being there."

Thomas shined his flashlight across the room to see the cabinet better. As he did, Jake noticed something that sent chills down his spine.

"Oh my gosh," Jake gasped. "There are fresh footprints in the dust on the floor. Are you sure you haven't been down here recently?"

"Yeah, I'm sure," Thomas shot back. "I told you I'm terrified of this place."

"Well, somebody has been down here very recently. See these shoe prints in the dust? If they were old, there would be a layer of dust on top of them."

Jake shined his light up the stairs. "Look," he said. "The footprints go up the stairs."

"Those are our footprints," Thomas scolded.

"No," Jake objected. "There are also footprints going up the stairs. Whoever was down here also went up the stairs."

Thomas began to tremble. "Should I call the police?" He asked.

"Maybe," Jake replied.

Despite the seven-year age difference, Jake seemed older than Thomas. It wasn't that he looked older. It was that he had experienced more in his life than his older brother. Jake had served four years in the army before going into construction. His temperament and military training made him more prone to action than Thomas.

He wasn't worried about the house being haunted; he was more practical than that. He was worried that there might be somebody hiding in the cabinet across the room. He shined his light around until he found the window. It was closed and locked on the inside. If somebody had been in the basement, they didn't come in through the window.

"This doesn't make any sense, Thomas," Jake said, trying to figure out who made the footprints if the basement had been locked up. "Are you sure nobody has been down here?"

Thomas was beginning to panic. "Yeah, I'm sure," he hissed. "I've kept the key in my pocket for years just because I'm so paranoid about this basement. Janet doesn't even have a key. I'm the only one with a key," he said, his voice elevating as he spoke.

"Okay, calm down," Jake said. "Let's just walk over to the cabinet and make sure there's nobody in it."

"I think I'm going to throw up," Thomas whined, his voice quivering with fear.

"Take it easy," Jake said, trying to calm his brother. "You just stay here and hold the flashlight. I'll walk over and open the cabinet."

"Okay," Thomas whispered. The panic he felt had almost taken his breath away.

Jake began walking toward the cabinet. Even though he felt it was irrational, he was having difficulty suppressing his fear. With each step he took, he felt his heart beating harder. Summoning all the courage he could muster; he picked up his pace and marched over to the cabinet. Just as he reached for the door handle, he heard someone scream for help upstairs. It was Mia's voice.

"Jake, Thomas," she cried. "Something's happening to Janet."

The brothers scrambled to the top of the stairs. No matter what was happening upstairs, it had to be less frightening than being in the basement with no lights.

They rushed out to the back patio where they found Thomas' wife lying on the floor, writhing. Her face had lost its natural color and had taken on a grayish hue.

"What happened?" Jake demanded.

"I don't know," Mia responded. "We were just sitting here, talking, and all of a sudden, Janet started convulsing. That's when I called you guys to come up."

Thomas stood still, frozen with fear. Jake told Mia to call 911 as he knelt beside Janet. He turned her head to the side to try to clear her air passage.

"Was she choking on something? Do we need to do the Heimlich?" Jake asked Mia.

"No, I don't think she was choking. She was talking and suddenly stopped. It's like her eyes rolled back and she started jerking. I helped her lay down, but she couldn't talk."

Mia relayed instructions from the 911 operator to Jake, who was frantically trying to save Janet's life. He began chest compressions and continued them until the paramedics arrived. They loaded Janet into the ambulance and took her to the emergency room. Thomas rode with them.

Jake and Mia put Tawny and Jeffrey into their car and drove around the block to their house. Mia took the kids inside and Jake continued to the hospital. He found Thomas in the waiting room. The older brother looked up at Jake with tears streaming down his cheeks.

"They couldn't save her, Jake," he said, choking on his words. "Janet's gone!"

Jake stood looking at Thomas in disbelief. Finally, he spoke. "Do they know what happened?"

"No," Thomas sobbed. "The doctor said that she might have had an allergic reaction to something she ate, but she didn't have any food allergies that I know of." He paused before continuing. "Something's not right here, Jake. Something's just not right."

"Mia took the kids to our house," Jake said. "Why don't you spend the night with us, and we'll figure this out in the morning?"

"I'm never going back to that house on the corner, Jake. I just can't be there anymore."

"Yeah, I don't blame you," said Jake. "A lot of bad memories in that house. C'mon, let's go home. You stay with us tonight."

Janet was laid to rest the following weekend. Her young children were still trying to understand why their mother was not coming home. Thomas and the children had been staying with Jake and Mia since Janet died. He had continued to refuse to go back to the house, so Jake and Mia made several trips to retrieve the family's necessities.

The funeral was an especially solemn occasion. After the service, the funeral party followed the hearse to the cemetery. During the graveside service, Jake noticed a man standing off in the distance, watching the group gathered at Janet's grave. Jake kept looking toward the man, trying to figure out who he was and why he was watching from a distance.

At the end of the graveside ceremony, the small group began to disperse. The man was still watching. Something about his presence disturbed Jake. Janet's death was suspicious and the man watching from a distance caused Jake to wonder why he wasn't part of the funeral party and if he had something to do with her death.

Jake decided to approach the man but as he walked toward him, the man turned and hurried away. Jake yelled at him to stop but the man began to run. Jake chased him but just as quickly as the man seemed to appear, he vanished.

As Jake returned to his family, Thomas asked what was going on.

"Did you see that guy that was watching us over there?" Jake said, pointing to the area where the man had been standing?

"No," Thomas responded, "I didn't see anybody."

"Well, I thought it was weird that he was watching us and didn't come over to join us. If he knew Janet, why wasn't he right here with us?"

"I don't know, bro," Thomas said, sourly. "You think he had something to do with…" He was emotionally unable to finish his thought.

"It's been a rough day," Mia said, trying to change the conversation. "Let's all go home."

Jake decided it was best to let it go. It was probably nothing.

Chapter Four

Distant Voices

Shortly after the funeral, Thomas and his two children moved into a new house. He refused to take any furniture from the old house, so he purchased new furniture for it. He swore he would never set foot in the house on the corner ever again, and he was staying true to his conviction. It was almost as if he blamed the house for his wife's death. Jake and Mia insisted that the kids needed their toys and clothes and agreed to get all their personal items from the house so Thomas wouldn't have to go inside.

One evening after work, they collected some boxes and drove Jake's truck around the block to the old house. As they walked up to the front door, Jake had a strange sensation that made the hair on the back of his neck stand on end. He paused. Mia took a few more steps before turning around.

"What's the matter?" she asked.

"I don't know," Jake said, "I just got the shivers thinking about the ghost stories Thomas and Janet were talking about last time we were here. The place just seems creepy now."

Mia smiled, reassuringly, "You don't really believe in ghosts, do you?" she asked.

"Well, I didn't until Janet died. Somehow that just makes the old place feel creepier."

Mia extended her hand and said, "C'mon, just put that out of your mind and let's get the job done."

Jake took her hand as she led him up to the front door. He pulled the key out of his pocket and turned it in the lock. The key turned freely with no resistance.

"The door isn't locked," he said, "We must have forgotten to lock it the day Janet died. None of us have been back here since then."

"The police have been here investigating," Mia replied. "They probably left it unlocked. I'm sure everything is fine, but we have to go in there and check, anyway."

Jake opened the door and stepped in cautiously. He turned on the light and looked around. Nothing seemed to be out of place. They walked into the kitchen. All the food and dishes from their barbeque were strewn about. The smell of spoiled food permeated the air. Neither Jake nor Mia had even thought about cleaning up after tragedy struck that night.

Mia sighed. "Maybe I should clean this up while you pack up Thomas and the kids' clothes and things."

Jake agreed. He picked up a few boxes and headed upstairs to the kids' rooms. He walked into 6-year-old Jeffrey's room and surveyed all the toys strewn about. As he began picking them up and packing them into boxes, he thought he heard the faint sound of children's voices, as if they were playing a game. He stopped working and listened, but the faint sound was gone. 'Maybe it was just extraneous sounds of loading the boxes,' he thought to himself. 'Or maybe it's just my imagination."

He continued loading Jeffrey's things into boxes. A short time later he thought he heard children's voices again, so he stopped his work and listened intently. This time the sound continued. It sounded like a little girl sobbing. He tiptoed through the upstairs bedrooms trying to determine where the sound was coming from. In some rooms the sobbing seemed a little louder, but he couldn't find the source. He didn't think there really was a little girl hiding in the house, but he was beginning to understand what his brother had been experiencing. He went downstairs to the kitchen where Mia was doing dishes.

"You're not done already, are you?" she asked.

"No," Jake replied, "I keep hearing the sound of children upstairs. Can you come up and see if you hear it?" he asked sheepishly.

Mia stopped cleaning and looked at Jake with a smirk on her face. "Are you really getting sucked into this haunted house thing?" she laughed.

"I don't know," Jake said, boyishly. "Maybe."

Mia looked at him for a moment, then said, "Okay, let's go."

Jake led her up the stairs and into Jeffrey's room.

"This is where I heard it," he said, looking around as if he was expecting to see something. They stood in the center of the room, quietly listening for the sound Jake had heard. Then the sound of a little girl singing softly touched Jake's ears. "Do you hear that?" he asked.

Mia tried listening more intently. "Hear what?" she asked.

"I hear a little girl singing. It's really faint, but I swear I can hear it."

Mia stood next to Jake, trying not to make any noise so she could hear the sound he was describing if there was one. Then she heard it; very faintly at first but as she listened it became a little louder.

"Oh my gosh!" Mia exclaimed in a whisper, "I think I hear it. It sounds like a little girl singing a lullaby."

The singing grew a little louder and both Jake and Mia could make out the words they heard the mysterious child's voice singing:

Hush, little baby don't say a word
Mama's gonna buy you a mockingbird
And if that mockingbird don't sing
Mama's gonna buy you a diamond ring

"This is really creepy," Mia whispered.

"Yeah," Jake whispered in reply.

"I can't believe we're hearing this," Mia said. "It's gotta be coming from somewhere in the house."

Mia began walking around the room, peaking in the closet, and behind the door. She got down on her hands and knees and looked under the bed. As she walked by the window that overlooked the backyard she stopped. Her eyes grew wide as she looked outside.

"Jake," she hissed, "look at this!"

Jake walked over and looked out the window. His attention was immediately drawn to the swing set in the backyard. Under the full moon he could clearly see that both swings were swinging but in opposite directions.

"No freaking way," Jake stammered as he took in the phenomenon.

"It can't be the wind doing that, right?" Mia asked.

"No," Jake replied. "If it was the wind, they would both be swinging the same direction at the same time."

"So, I guess the place really is haunted," Mia said.

"Seems that way," Jake replied.

"Well, we have to get Thomas and the kids' stuff, cause they're not coming over here," Mia said with a sigh. "And at this point I don't blame them."

The front door slammed. Their eyes widened as they looked at each other. A door creaked open downstairs, followed by footsteps descending the stairs to the basement.

"Somebody just came into the house!" Jake gasped.

Mia nodded. Her eyes were wide with fright.

Jake grabbed a baseball bat that was lying on the floor and walked cautiously out to the landing. He peered down at the first-floor entryway.

"Hello?" he called out. "Who's down there?" he demanded.

Nobody answered. He and Mia cautiously walked downstairs, expecting to find an intruder. They edged toward the basement door. It was partially open. Jake paused.

"Do you think it's a ghost, or a person?" he asked.

"After what we saw and heard upstairs, I don't know," Mia replied.

They approached the door and looked down the stairs. The dusty steps with footprints that Jake and Thomas had encountered on the day Janet died were now clean. Not just from the police walking up and down them while they were investigating her death, but it looked like somebody had swept them clean. Jake opened the door a little wider and looked down the stairs. Suddenly he realized that the lights in the stairwell were working. Somebody had replaced them. He nudged Mia and pointed to the stairwell.

"Look," he said. "The lights have been replaced."

"So?" Mia replied.

"When Thomas and I went down to the basement last time we were here, all the lights down there were burned out. Somebody has replaced them and cleaned the stairs."

"Maybe the police did," Mia replied.

"Maybe."

"What if somebody is down there?" Mia asked.

"Well, I guess we better find out."

With bat in hand Jake led the way down the stairs. When they reached the bottom, he cautiously peered around the corner into the basement. It was a single room with no obstructions. There wasn't anybody in sight, and everything seemed to be the same as it was the last time he had been down there, except the cabinet that had been there before was gone.

"I think somebody has been taking stuff from the house," Jake said, relaxing a little. Pointing to the other side of the room, he continued. "There was a cabinet over on that wall by that old bookcase when Thomas and I came down here. Now it's gone."

"I'm not worried about stolen property right now, Jake," Mia said with mild annoyance. "Somebody entered through the front door and came down to the basement. Where are they now?"

"Well, they're not down here," Jake replied with a hint of sarcasm. "And there's nowhere to hide down here."

They went back upstairs, determined to find the intruder, if there was one. They walked through the kitchen and into the dining room, then circled back through the drawing room and entryway. They walked down the hall to the parlor, then checked the first-floor bathroom. Nobody was on the first floor. They climbed the stairs back up to the second floor and searched all the bedrooms and bathrooms. Finally, they checked the attic but didn't find anyone in the house.

As they walked down the hall toward the top of the stairs, they became aware of a regular creaking sound coming from one of the upstairs bedrooms. They both stopped.

"What's that sound?" Mia whispered.

"I don't know," Jake replied in a low voice. "It sounds like it's coming from Tawny's room."

They crept back to the room and peered inside. An old rocking chair in the corner that had been in the house for decades was rocking back and forth. But nobody was sitting on it.

The sight filled the couple with terror. They looked at each other, then bolted downstairs and out the door, leaving it wide open. They ran down the walkway to Jake's truck. He already had the engine running by the time Mia slid into the passenger seat.

"Jake," she panted. "We left the door open."

"I don't care," Jake replied as he put the truck in gear.

Mia put her hand on his arm. "We can't leave the door open, Jake," she said with an authoritative tone.

He put the truck in park and turned toward his wife. "So, I have to go close it, right?" he whined.

Mia patted him on the back and said, "You got this, Jake!"

Jake obediently got out of the truck and trudged up to the door. He grabbed the handle, slammed it shut and locked it as fast as he could. Then he turned and bolted back to his truck.

Mia was the first one to speak as they sped away from the house. "Do you think that Janet is haunting the house?" she asked.

"I don't know," Jake answered. "Maybe."

They drove in silence for a while. Instead of driving home, Jake was driving toward Thomas' house.

"Where are we going?" Mia asked when she realized they were not driving home.

"I thought we should talk to Thomas about this."

Mia agreed. They drove the rest of the way in silence. Thomas was surprised to find them at his door and invited them in. They sat in the living room as Mia and Jake recounted everything that had happened at the old house.

"Now you see why I'm not going back to that horrible house," Thomas said after hearing about their supernatural encounters.

"The thing that bothers me the most," Jake said, "is that the cabinet that was in the basement is gone."

"I didn't even know there was a cabinet before you and I went down there," Thomas said, shaking his head. "I really don't care if somebody stole it."

"Yeah, but why didn't they take anything else?" Jake asked.

"Don't know, Bro," Thomas replied. "Don't care. That house can burn to the ground for all I care."

"We still need to get your stuff out of there," Mia said. "How are we going to do that?"

"We don't need any of that stuff," Thomas said, waving his hand.

"But the kids do," Mia countered. "They need their toys and clothes."

"We'll go buy new stuff," Thomas said, cutting her off.

"I'm good with that," Jake said, getting up out of his chair.

Jake and Mia drove home in silence. Neither knew what to say after their experience at the old house. And neither was in a hurry to go back to it.

Chapter Five

The Fixer Upper

The door creaked on its hinges as it slowly swung open. Jake stood outside with his tool bag in hand, thinking of all the bad memories the house elicited. A year had passed since the last time he was there but the supernatural encounters he and Mia experienced, and the death of his sister-in-law were still fresh in his mind.

Thomas was still distressed about losing his wife there and was adamant that he would never cross its threshold again. In fact, he had started referring to his former residence as 'the house on the corner,' trying to separate himself completely from it. He had asked Jake to fix the house up so he could sell it, but Jake had been procrastinating because of the weird experiences and bad memories of the house.

Thomas had recently become engaged to a much younger woman he had only been dating for several months. He wanted to sell the house before he got married.

Jake's heart began racing as he stepped across the threshold. He paused just inside the door. He realized that he had to get the job done, so he shook the thoughts away and closed the front door. It was daytime after all. Ghost stuff just happens at night. At least that's what he told himself.

He decided to start in the basement and work his way up to the second floor. His first task was to change the old skeleton key lock on the basement door to a new standard key. With that task completed, he trudged down the stairs to see what needed to be repaired. He reached the bottom and peered around the corner into the empty room. To his surprise, the old cabinet was back. He was immediately seized with fear as he looked at it. Why was it there when he and Thomas went down the night Janet died, and gone the next time he went back to the house with Mia?

Mustering as much courage as he could, he walked across the floor to examine it. He never had the chance to open it when he and Thomas went down there, and he was curious about what was inside it. Fear began welling up inside him as he wondered if somebody might be hiding in it. Pushing down his fears, he reached for the door, jerked it open and jumped back.

The cabinet was empty except for a strange looking box with two bars sticking out of it. Jake reached in to pick up the box, but it wouldn't move. It seemed to be stuck to the cabinet. He had never seen anything like it. He picked up his phone and called his brother.

"Hey bro, what's up?" Thomas said, answering his phone.

"I'm down in the basement of the old house and that cabinet is back."

"What cabinet?" Thomas asked, pretending he had no memory of it.

"The cabinet that was here when you and I came down and gone the next time Mia and I came down here, remember?" Jake said, impatiently.

"Yeah, I guess I have a vague recollection of that," Thomas said. "Why?"

"Well, I opened it up and there's a weird metal box inside with a couple of goofy handles attached to it. There's also a couple of meters and dials and some lights on it like it's used to measure something. Have you ever seen it before?"

Jake's question was met with silence. After a moment's pause, he asked, "Thomas, are you there?"

"Yeah, dude. I told you before, I never went down in the basement except that one time with Dad and the time with you. I don't even remember seeing a cabinet down there."

"Oh, okay," Jake replied.

The silence on the other end of the phone was awkward. Jake realized that he was bringing up painful memories of the day Thomas lost his wife. "Thomas, I'm sorry I brought this up," he stammered. "I'm gonna hang up now and get to work on the place. Love ya, bro."

Thomas didn't respond. Jake ended the call and went upstairs to work. He skipped the main floor and went up to the second floor to fix a leaky faucet in the bathroom. While he was hunched over the sink, he thought he heard a little girl humming. It was a strange sound, almost like it was coming from another dimension. He stopped his work to focus in on the sound. Just then, a little girl walked into the bathroom. Startled, Jake jumped back and gasped.

The girl looked to be around ten or eleven. She had long blond hair that was tied back in a ponytail. She didn't seem to notice that Jake was there and went straight to the sink to wash her hands. Jake had taken the faucet apart to repair it, but the girl didn't seem to notice. As she reached out to turn on the water, the faucet changed. The parts Jake had taken off flew back into place and water began flowing. The girl put her hands under the water and rubbed them together. As she finished and turned the water off, the parts Jake had taken off fell silently back to the counter.

The girl dried her hands and began walking out of the bathroom, never acknowledging Jake's presence.

"Hey little girl," Jake called out. "What are you doing here? How did you get in here?"

The girl didn't respond. She walked through the adjoining bedroom and out the door. Just then, Jake heard a woman's voice downstairs.

"Annie, are you coming to dinner?" the voice called out. Like the girl's voice, it sounded distant.

"Yes, mother, I'm coming," the girl replied.

Jake followed the girl downstairs into the dining room where a teenage boy and middle-aged man sat at the table. The woman soon came out of the kitchen and sat at the table, which was prepared with place settings. A pot roast sat in a large tray in the center of the table. The man put his paper away and said, "Smells wonderful, Honey. Let's dig in."

The family observed a formality that Jake had not seen since his youth. The table had been set with plates, and a napkin on the left of the plate. A fork was set on top of the napkin. A knife was placed on the right side of the plate with a spoon next to it. Jake had been taught how to set a table like this, but he and Mia had adopted a less formal meal etiquette.

As Jake watched the family eating dinner, he suddenly realized that these people were dressed a little odd. He should have picked up on it when he noticed the man reading a newspaper. Nobody had a cell phone. Their clothes looked vintage, but he couldn't place the era they were from. An old-fashioned rotary dial phone hung on the wall. There was a strange, otherworldly look to the family, almost like they were not in the same dimension as Jake. Not to mention that he could not smell the pot roast that sat on the table in front of him.

The family did not notice Jake staring at them. After his encounter with the girl in the bathroom, he didn't even try to communicate with them. But as he watched them at the dining room table, they all vanished, and the sound of their conversation trailed off into the distance until it was silent.

Jake didn't waste any time getting out of the house. His exit was so swift that he almost didn't lock the front door. As he raced down the front walk to his truck that was parked on the street, his phone rang. It was Thomas.

"Jake," Thomas said, sounding distraught. "I've been arrested. They think I killed Janet. I need you to come down to the police station."

While he drove to the police station, Jake's thoughts bounced back and forth between Thomas' arrest and what he had just seen in the old house. He was distressed to think that the authorities suspected Thomas of murder, but the things he had just experienced in the house on the corner were also troubling.

The family he saw must have been some kind of ghostly apparition. The fact that it happened in broad daylight didn't make it less scary as he thought about it. The last time he had encountered ghosts in the house was at night. In fact, all the ghost stories he had ever heard always happened at night. Why did this happen during the day?

He arrived at the police station and walked into the lobby. Thomas was in an interrogation room. Two detectives were questioning him about Janet. One of them saw Jake through the window and came out to talk to him.

"Your brother is not under arrest," the detective explained. "He's just been brought in for questioning. Our investigation has determined that his wife was poisoned and we're trying to find out who did that. Naturally, your brother is high on the list of possible suspects."

"Thomas would never hurt anybody, especially his wife," Jake said, clearly annoyed at the accusation. "He loved her, and he was devastated by her death."

"Why don't we go into another room where we can have some privacy, Mr. Holden."

Jake rolled his eyes. "My name is Holman, by the way. Not Holden," he said as he followed the detective down the hall into an office.

The detective motioned for Jake to sit in a chair in front of a desk, then walked around the desk and sat down on the other side. He shuffled through some papers for a few minutes before talking.

"An autopsy found traces of Strychnine poisoning in Mrs. Holden's body," the detective said, looking at one of the papers. "The coroner said that she probably consumed it about the time the family ate dinner. The lab found traces of poison in one of the glasses, most likely the one the victim drank from." The detective leaned back in his chair and fixed his gaze on Jake. "To the best of your recollection, Mr. Holden, what happened that night?"

Jake looked at the officer for a moment before answering. "First of all, it's Holman. And second, Janet died nearly a year ago. Why are you just looking into this now?"

The officer took a deep breath and sighed. "Your sister-in-law's death has been under investigation since it happened," he said with some irritation in his voice. "It takes a while to get reports back on the autopsy and other investigations that have been running. Now, to the best of your recollection, what happened the night Mrs. Holden died?"

"It's Holman! And I honestly don't know," Jake said. "We ate dinner and afterward my brother and I went down to the basement to look at something. Then we heard my wife screaming and ran upstairs where we found Janet laying on the ground. I think she was probably dead before we even got outside."

The officer continued his line of questioning. "Are you aware of any instances of abuse or domestic violence between your brother and his wife?"

Jake shook his head in disbelief. Thomas had never been violent. Even as a child he refused to watch Looney Toons cartoons because the fighting upset him. He disliked sports because of the competition. He felt bad that somebody had to lose.

"My brother is the most docile person I know," Jake responded. "He would never hurt anyone."

"Are you aware that Mrs. Holden had—"

"It's HOLMAN, you stupid idiot," Jake yelled, jumping out of his chair and pointing his finger across the desk at the detective. "How hard is it to get somebody's name right?"

The detective lurched back in his chair in response to Jake's aggressive outburst. His face expressed surprise at the sudden change in demeanor. Then a wry smile crossed the detective's lips. Jake realized that he had just played into the detective's ploy to get him angry. The mispronunciation of his name was just a tactic to see how he would react.

"You've got a pretty hot temper," the detective said with a grin. "Does that run in your family? Does Thomas have a hidden temper like that?"

Jake flopped back in his chair and shook his head. "Thomas is nothing like me."

The detective continued his line of questioning. "Are you aware that your sister-in-law had scars on the back of her head consistent with having been hit with a blunt object in the past? Or that she had scars on her back consistent with stab wounds?"

Jake was dumbfounded. "No. I had no idea. Are you sure you have the right body?"

The detective sat behind the desk with his finger on his cheek and stared at Jake for a long time. "Yeah," he finally said. "We have the right body. The coroner says that the scars on Janet's body are consistent with some pretty brutal events. According to his report, whatever left those scars should have killed her."

Again, the detective sat and stared at Jake, who continued squirming in his chair.

Finally, Jake broke the awkward silence. "So, where are you going with this? Am I in trouble for something? I don't have any answers for the questions you're asking, and I'm totally blown away to learn about these scars Janet had?"

"Are you aware of any accidents the victim may have had that would account for the scars?

Jake thought for a moment. "No. I've known Janet since childhood, and I don't remember her ever being in an accident."

"Do you know how we can get in touch with her parents?" the officer asked.

Jake paused. "They were killed in a car accident a few years ago."

"But Janet was not with them?"

"No," Jake said, recalling the horrific accident that took the life of Janet's parents. "She was going to go with them on a camping trip but ended up not going. I don't remember why. While they were driving up in the mountains, their car lost a wheel and veered off a steep hill. Her parents and her younger brother were all killed."

"What about your wife?" the detective pried. "She was the only one with Janet the day she died."

"She had nothing to do with it," Jake sputtered, defensively.

"Sure about that?" the detective asked, smugly.

"Yeah, I'm sure."

"Tell me about your wife's family? What kind a people are they?"

Jake fidgeted nervously. The question made him uncomfortable. Did the detective know something about Mia's family that he didn't?

"I don't know anything about her family," he finally confessed. "She doesn't have any siblings and her parents died before I met her."

"I see," the detective smirked. "How did her parents die?"

"Some kind of industrial accident. What does this have to do with Janet?"

"I don't know. That's what I'm trying to figure out. It seems that everybody around your little group is dead. Janet's parents, your wife's parents, and according to your brother, even your parents are dead."

"My parents died of natural causes," Jake protested heatedly.

The officer leaned back in his chair and continued to stare at Jake. After another long, awkward period of silence, Jake finally said, "Um, are we done?"

"Not quite," the officer said. "Your brother is apparently engaged to be married. How long has he been seeing this new woman?"

Jake shook his head. "Just a few months," he said.

"I understand that she's a much younger woman. Is that correct?"

"Yes."

"Is it possible that your brother killed his wife so that he can be with this new, younger woman?"

Jake shook his head and sighed. "You really don't know my brother and you're really starting to tick me off, so unless you're going to arrest me, we're done!"

The officer's eyes narrowed as he stared at Jake. Finally, he said, "Yeah, I guess I don't have any more questions for you at this time."

"What about my brother? What's going to happen to him?"

"Well, we don't have enough evidence to hold him…yet, so I guess you can take him home; at least for now."

The detective escorted Jake back to the lobby where he waited until Thomas was escorted out of the interrogation room. The brothers walked out of the police station to the parking lot. Jake was surprised to see that it was dark outside. The interviews must have lasted longer than he thought. Thomas was silent as they walked across the parking lot.

"Are you okay?" Jake asked as they climbed into his truck.

Thomas began sobbing. "They think I killed Janet," he said through his tears. "How can they think I could do that?"

"I don't know," Jake said. "Something is very weird about all this."

"And they said that Janet had some scars on her back," Thomas continued. "I never saw any scars on her back."

"Yeah," said Jake. "They brought that up with me too. It makes me wonder if they did the autopsy on the wrong body."

They drove in silence for a few minutes, then Thomas asked, "Do you think I need a lawyer, Jake?"

"I don't know. Maybe we need to hire a private investigator to look into this, to try to figure out what's going on."

Jake pulled up to Thomas' house and turned off the engine.

"Thomas, it's going to be okay," Jake said, trying to reassure his brother. "We'll get through this together." He said the words, but he wasn't sure if he believed them. Things had gotten very weird.

Jake walked Thomas to the door, where his fiancé, Bridget, was waiting with the door open.

"I finally got the kids to bed, but they're really worried about you," Bridget said as they approached the door.

"Yeah, it's been a rough day," Thomas said as he hugged her. "Thanks for watching them."

"I called Mia to let her know what's going on," Bridget said to Jake.

"Thanks," He replied.

Jake wished them both a good night, got in his truck and drove home. His mind was reeling from the events of the day. Mia had been trying to call him, but he hadn't taken her call because of the police interrogation. He had a lot to tell her, but he wasn't in much of a mood to talk. She met him at the door when he got home.

"I was getting worried," she said as she reached out to hug him.

"They arrested Thomas for murder," Jake muttered.

"Yeah, Bridget called me. Is Thomas in jail?"

"No, they didn't actually arrest him, they just took him in for questioning and let him go. I just dropped him off at his house."

"I can't believe this," Mia exclaimed. "Thomas wouldn't hurt a fly."

"Yeah, that's what I told them," Jake replied.

"So, they talked to you too?"

Jake told her about his conversation with the police officer, about the scars they allegedly found on Janet's body and that she apparently was poisoned. After he finished talking, the couple sat in silence for a few minutes. Finally, Mia broke the silence.

"There's some dinner in the fridge."

"I'm not really hungry," Jake said.

"It's been a long day," she said. "Let's go to bed."

Chapter Six

Time Warp

The next morning, Jake's alarm sounded at 5:30 AM. He punched the snooze button and rolled over to sleep a little longer.

"You know that's not a good idea!" Mia said. She was already up, had already showered and was standing in front of the bathroom mirror putting on her makeup. Jake dragged himself out of bed and stumbled into the bathroom.

"Good morning, Honey," she said cheerily.

"Morning," Jake grunted, wiping the sleep out of his eyes.

Mia was always up before Jake. She didn't like to feel rushed while she got ready in the morning and if Jake happened to be ready before her, he would pace the floor while he waited. She hated that so she made it a point to get up before him.

Jake showered and dressed. Mia had breakfast waiting when he came downstairs. He gobbled it down, kissed his wife and headed out the door. On his way to the construction site, he passed the house on the corner.

Despite the terrible events that had happened there recently, Jake couldn't help reminiscing every time he passed his childhood home.

Nobody had been living in it since Thomas' wife passed away and it was showing signs of neglect.

Jake's thoughts were interrupted by his cell phone. He tapped the blue tooth earpiece and answered the call.

"Jake," said the voice on the other end. "It's Thomas."

"Hey Thomas," Jake replied. "Everything okay?"

"Yeah, I guess. I'm still really weirded out about the police thing yesterday, but I'm trying to stay positive."

"I'm glad to hear that," Jake said. "So, what's up?"

"I'm calling about the house on the corner," Thomas began.

"Yeah, I know," Jake said. "I need to get it fixed up so you can sell it."

"Well… actually, I just rented it out. Some guy called me up out of the blue and said he wanted to rent it for two months."

"I'm not sure that's a good idea, Thomas," Jake replied. "It's not in great shape."

"I know, and I told the guy it had some problems, but he didn't care. He was really stuck on renting the house, so I finally agreed. He's moving in right away."

Something felt odd to Jake. "Why would he want to rent the house when there are problems with it?" he asked.

"Oh, come on, Jake. It's not that bad. I was living there up until…" His voice trailed off, but Jake knew what he was going to say.

Thomas had rarely talked about Janet since her death. He still hadn't come to terms with it, even though he was now engaged to be married again. Jake worried that he was just marrying to have somebody to watch his kids while he was at work, a kind of built-in daycare arrangement.

"Anyway," Thomas continued. "You won't have to worry about the remodel for a few months. Gotta go, Bridget is waiting for me."

Bridget was ten years younger than Thomas. She was bubbly and talkative, and just a little bit giddy. Jake and Mia had mixed feelings about her. They wondered what she saw in an older, out of shape man, which made them suspicious of her motives.

The wedding was three months away. Secretly, Mia and Jake hoped that Thomas would call it off, but that was unlikely. They were afraid that both Bridget and Thomas were getting married for the wrong reasons.

Jake had several construction sites to check on. As he made his rounds, he kept thinking of the old house on the corner. The renovations it needed were only part of the problem. The supernatural occurrences were far more worrisome now that a renter was involved.

Jake met Mia for lunch at noon. They dined at their favorite burger shop that had been around for generations and still had the look and feel of a bygone era. They had just ordered and were waiting for their food when Jake's phone rang. It wasn't a number he was familiar with.

"Hi Jake, this is Zander Knox," the voice on the phone said. "I'm renting the house from your brother. Thomas gave me your number and suggested I call you."

"Yeah, he just mentioned you were renting the house this morning. Is there something wrong?"

"Well, there's something a little odd here that I wanted to show you. Could you stop by sometime?"

Bizarre might have been a better word, considering the strange experience Jake had in the house just the day before and the scary events he and Mia had experienced nearly a year ago. Jake suspected that the new renter must have had some supernatural experience he wanted to talk about.

"Yeah, I can come by on my way home this afternoon. Would that work?"

"That would be fine," Zander replied. "I'll see you then."

Jake hung up the phone and looked at Mia. She had a questioning look in her eye.

"What was that about?" She asked.

"Oh… uh, Thomas just rented out his old house. That was the tenant. He said there's something weird at the house he wanted me to look at."

"Something weird? That's an understatement," Mia said.

"No kidding."

"When did Thomas rent it out? I thought it needed some work."

"Yeah, it was kind of sudden. He called me this morning and told me about it. Then he rushed off to meet Bridget. I guess they're getting the wedding all planned out."

"He didn't say what the problem was?"

"Who, the renter?"

"Yeah."

"No, I guess I'll find out when I get there. I'm hoping there's something going on with the plumbing or maybe rats have chewed through some of the electrical wires. I'd rather not experience anymore weird stuff."

"What do you know about this guy?" Mia asked. "Is he okay?"

"I don't know anything about him, but knowing Thomas, he probably just saw money and didn't think about a background check or anything."

They finished their lunch and kissed as they parted. Mia went back to her school class and Jake went back to his job site. At about 5:00 PM, he loaded up his tools and headed home. He had forgotten about the conversation with the new renter until he rounded the corner and came up to the entrance of his neighborhood. When the house on the corner came into view, he remembered that he was supposed to stop by.

As he approached, he saw several kids playing in the front yard. 'That's kind of odd,' he thought to himself. 'I didn't realize the renter had kids.'

As he came nearer to the house, a chill went down his spine. The kids playing in the front yard were his niece and nephew – Thomas' kids. Somehow, they looked younger than the last time he saw them. He dismissed the spine-tingling sensation, thinking that Thomas must be there, despite his refusal to ever set foot in the house again. An uneasy feeling began welling up inside him when he saw Janet's car parked in the driveway. Thomas had sold the car after her death, but there it was back at their old house. As he pulled up in front of the house, the kids ran up to his car to greet him.

"Hi, Uncle Jake," little Jeffrey said.

"Hi guys, is your dad inside?"

"No," Jeffrey replied. "He hasn't come home from work, yet. Mom is in the kitchen, though."

The tingle down Jake's spine returned. He didn't understand what his nephew meant since the boy's mother had been dead for nearly a year. He wasn't quite sure how to approach the situation.

"What do you mean, your mom is in the house?" he finally asked.

"Mom's in the kitchen making dinner," Jeffrey said. "Are you and Aunt Mia coming over?"

"Jeffrey, your mother is…" Jake's voice trailed off as he looked up at the house and saw Janet through the kitchen window.

"That's not possible!" He muttered to himself in amazement. He walked up to the front door, escorted by his niece and nephew. His senses were screaming to leave but he was paralyzed with fear. Something was definitely not right. It wasn't possible for his sister-in-law to be here. She was dead, so who was this person in the house that looked just like her? And why were his niece and nephew acting like everything was normal?

The children opened the door and pushed Jake into the house.

"Mom," Jeffrey called out. "Uncle Jake's here."

Janet came out of the kitchen with a smile on her face. "Hi Jake, where's Mia?"

Jake stood still, staring at Janet in disbelief. After a moment of awkwardness, Janet broke the silence.

"Are you okay, Jake?" She asked.

"Wha-What?" Jake replied, shaking his head, trying to clear his thoughts. "Oh, Mia's at home," he said nervously. "I just stopped by because…" He broke off mid-sentence, not knowing how to finish.

They stared at each other for a few moments. Jake's mind was racing. Finally, he asked, "Janet, how are you here? How is this possible?"

"How is what possible?" Janet asked, confused.

Jake hesitated again, trying to understand what was happening. "Where is Thomas?" he finally asked.

"He called and said he's running a little late. Did you forget you and Mia were coming over for dinner tonight?"

"Dinner?" Jake stammered. "Tonight?"

"Yeah," Janet replied. "We invited you guys over for dinner tonight. I thought that's why you were here."

Jake stood motionless, staring at Janet as though she was a ghost. In fact, he was pretty sure she was a ghost. She died a year ago. He and Mia went to the funeral. Thomas and the kids had moved out of the house after her death and Thomas was engaged to another woman. Now Janet was back acting like nothing had happened.

"Are you sure you're okay, Jake?" Janet said after a moment. "You're acting really weird."

Jake decided to play along while he tried to figure out what was happening, "Sorry Janet," he finally replied. "I guess I forgot all about dinner tonight. I'll go get Mia and be right back."

He walked to the front door and looked back into the house. Something was different. The house seemed newer. It was in better shape than it had been the last time he was there. It was just like it was when Thomas and his family lived in it.

Thomas arrived home as Jake walked down the walkway to his truck. Jake approached him as he got out of his car.

"Hey bro," Thomas said as he opened his car door.

"What's going on, Thomas?" Jake asked sternly.

"You guys are coming for dinner, right?" Thomas answered.

"No, I mean, what's going on? Something weird is going on here."

"I'm not following you little brother."

"You called me this morning and said that you had a renter for the house. Your renter even called at lunch and asked me to come by this afternoon, so I showed up to check out the house before the renter moves in and I find your family here, including Janet. I'm totally freaked out by all this."

Thomas stared at Jake for a moment with a blank expression on his face. "I didn't call you this morning, Jake," he began slowly. "And I don't have a renter. Why would I rent this place out? We live here."

"Thomas, you haven't lived here for almost a year. After Janet died, you never wanted to be in the house, and…" Jake stopped talking as he saw the look on his brother's face turn to panic.

"What happened to Janet?" Thomas demanded. "Is she alright?" He brushed past Jake and hurried into the house. Jake followed, bewildered and without words to express his thoughts. Thomas burst through the front door and called his wife's name.

"I'm in the kitchen," Janet called back to him. She continued without realizing that Jake was there with Thomas. "Jake came over a few minutes ago and he was acting really strange. He looked at me like he'd seen a ghost." She looked up and saw Jake standing behind Thomas. "Oh, hi Jake," she said sheepishly.

Thomas turned to look at Jake and raised an eyebrow. "What the heck, bro?" he said. "Everything is fine here."

Jake stood silent for a moment trying to make sense of the situation. "I'm sorry," he said finally. "I feel like I'm trapped in a bad dream. I don't know how to explain myself. I'll go get Mia and we'll be back in a few minutes."

He turned and walked out of the house and down the walkway to his truck. He drove around the block to his home and walked through the door. Mia was in the kitchen preparing dinner. She looked up and noticed the strange expression on Jake's face.

"Hey Sweetie, everything okay?"

"I don't know," Jake said blankly. "I stopped by Thomas' house on the corner and as I drove up, I saw his' kids playing outside."

"So, was Thomas at the house? I thought he said he would never go back there."

"Yeah, he did. And yeah, he was at the house." He paused as he contemplated his next statement. "And… Janet was there too."

Mia cocked her head and squinted her eyes. "Honey," she began slowly and cautiously. "Janet died months ago."

"Yeah," Jake replied. "That's what I thought. But she was at their old house on the corner just five minutes ago. I talked to her. She said that they were expecting us for dinner."

Mia sat down at the table and thought for a moment before speaking. "Honey? Did you hit your head at work today?"

Jake laughed. "No."

"You know that Janet couldn't be at that house today, right?"

"Yes, I know that," he said weakly. "But she was."

The couple sat in silence for a while. Mia worried that Jake was having a breakdown, but she wasn't sure what to do about it. Finally, she had an idea.

"Come on, honey. Let's go over to the house. We'll figure out what's going on together."

They walked down the block in silence. As they rounded the corner and the house came into view, Jake immediately noticed that something about it was distinctly different than when he was there earlier. There were no kids playing outside. No cars in the driveway. No toys on the front lawn as there had been only minutes earlier. The house seemed to have slipped back into its more recent state of decay as well.

Jake led the way to the front door and knocked. Nobody answered. He slowly turned the doorknob. To his surprise, the house was not locked. The door creaked and groaned as it slowly swung inward to expose the home's dusty interior. He turned to look at Mia. She looked back at him with an expectant expression on her face. Jake grimaced.

"It was different a few minutes ago, I swear!"

He turned and walked through the door. He pointed toward the kitchen area and said, "Janet was standing right there in the kitchen. She was making dinner." Hearing no reply from Mia, he turned around. She was gone. The doorway was empty. "Mia?" He said, looking around. "Mia, where are you?"

Jake could hear the faint sound of Mia's voice calling him. She sounded far away and muffled. Suddenly, he was startled by a voice behind him.

"Jake, where's Mia? I thought you went to get her." It was Janet. She was standing in the doorway to the kitchen with an oven mitt over her hand.

"Uh, she's right outside," Jake stammered. "I know this sounds crazy, but when I walked into the house, she..." He paused, realizing how crazy it all sounded.

Without saying another word, he turned back toward the door and walked through it. As he stepped across the threshold to the outside, Mia was standing there, looking puzzled.

"What happened, Jake? You walked through that door, and you just disappeared."

"Mia," Jake said hurriedly. "Janet is on the other side of that door. Come on, let me show you."

Jake turned and walked back through the door. He called to Janet, but she didn't answer. He turned to talk to Mia, but she wasn't there. The house was empty, and Mia was gone.

Chapter Seven

Zander Knox

"Mia?" Jake called out. "Mia, where are you?"

Jake took a step toward the front door, but was interrupted by a deep, raspy male voice behind him.

"I expected you to come alone."

Jake turned to find a man behind him. He was an older man, perhaps in his late 50s. He had a well-groomed beard and shoulder-length hair that was just beginning to grey. Despite his distinguished appearance, the man had a bit of a rugged look. He stepped forward and extended his hand.

"I'm Zander Knox. I spoke with you on the phone earlier today."

Jake stared at him with his mouth open momentarily before regaining his composure and accepting Zander's extended hand.

"Oh, yeah," Jake said. "Sorry, it's been a really weird day."

"I'll bet it has," Zander replied.

"I know this sounds crazy, but I seemed to have lost my wife," Jake explained. "We came here together and…now she's not here."

"She's right there," Zander said with a wry smile, pointing toward the front door.

Jake turned toward the door. Mia was not there. He turned back to Zander, eyeing him suspiciously.

"She's…she's not there. Why would you say she's there?" He stammered.

Zander chuckled. "I wasn't expecting you to bring your wife, but I assure you, she's standing right there. She's just not in the same here and now as you." He paused, waiting to see if Jake understood what was happening. Then he continued. "Look at the house you're standing in, Jake. Does it look like the house as you know it?"

Jake looked around the house. He hadn't noticed before, but it was different. It looked like it had been completely renovated. Everything looked brand new.

"What the…" Jake muttered under his breath. "What's going on?" He demanded.

"Jake, listen to me very carefully. I want you to walk over to the front door but don't go outside."

Jake was wary, but he finally followed Zander's instructions and walked back to the door.

"Now," said Zander. "Call Mia's name, then be quiet and listen."

Jake turned back toward the open door and called out to Mia. He faintly heard her reply, as if she were far away or behind a wall.

"Jake?" she called back with a hint of fear in her voice. "Jake, where are you?"

"I'm inside the house."

"I'm inside the house too," she called back. "I can't find you. Where are you?"

Jake looked back at Zander for an explanation. "Where is she?" he asked.

"Not where, Jake, but when," Zander replied.

"What do you mean, when?" Jake demanded.

"Jake, I need you to remain calm as I explain this to you," Zander began.

Jake looked at Zander expectantly.

Zander continued, "You came over here earlier and found you brother's wife alive, right?"

"Yeah," Jake answered with suspicion. "How do you know that?

"Because I set it up so that you would experience that," Zander said. "I needed you to experience time travel firsthand, so that you would believe what I'm going to tell you."

"Okay, you have my attention," Jake said. "But first, can you bring my wife back?"

"All in good time," Zander answered. "I need to explain some things to you. When we're done, we'll go back in time to before you brought Mia over here, and she won't even remember that she came here."

Jake eyed Zander suspiciously. "Who are you?" he demanded.

"As I said before, my name is Zander Knox and I'm from the future."

Jake looked at Zander in disbelief. "Time travel is not possible."

"Oh, yes, it is," Zander responded confidently. "In fact, some of the early experiments in time travel started in your generation with simulations of sending particles back in time."

Zander paused waiting for Jake to object, but he didn't say anything. He just stared at Zander with a bewildered expression on his face.

"I'm a genetic physicist," Zander continued. "My team and I discovered a way to time travel using DNA. We're still learning a lot about it but basically this house is my time machine. My family built this house, Jake. You and I are distant relatives."

"No way!" Jake said.

"You need to believe it. Your life and the lives of your family members depend on it. Jake, your family is in danger. That's why I'm here. One hundred and fifty years in the future a murder will be committed in this house. The perpetrator escaped through time. I came to track him down and take him back to our time to stand trial."

Jake cleared his throat and swallowed. "So, the murderer is time traveling and you're chasing him through time?"

"Yes," Zander replied. "That's what I just said. And the murderer in the future, also killed your sister-in-law."

Jake thought back to the horrible night when Thomas' wife died. "So, you're saying that the killer you're chasing through time poisoned Janet?"

"Exactly right," Zander answered.

"Why would he travel 150 years back in time to kill her? That doesn't make any sense."

"It makes perfect sense if you know all the details. It turns out that the killer is descended from you, and I am Thomas' descendent.

Since we share the same essential DNA, we can both travel through time in this house.

"My scientific team and I had been using this house to experiment with time travel, because the house had been in the family for generations. We discovered that I could time travel as far back as our family has been in the house. During our experiments a distant relative of mine broke into the house to steal some expensive family heirlooms. His name is Derek Killian. He's always been a small time criminal. We don't know exactly what he was after, but his burglary attempt was apparently interrupted by someone who caught him in the house that night. A struggle ensued and Derek killed the man."

"What does that have to do with me and my family?" Jake asked.

"The house was set up for time travel at the time. In his attempt to get away, Derek inadvertently stumbled into the time module and escaped capture by making a time jump. I've been chasing him, trying to catch him and take back to our time to stand trial."

Jake eyed Zander with suspicion. He didn't want to believe what was happening, but the evidence was compelling. What else could explain Janet being back in the house a year after her death?

"That still doesn't explain what any of this has to do with me."

"When I came to the house the morning after the murder, the police were here investigating the crime. They couldn't figure it out. I realized that Derek must be related and therefore could escape through time in the house, because nobody but family members who share our DNA can time travel in this house. Since I'm the only one that can track him through time, I had no choice but to go after him.

"I've almost caught him several times, but he has always managed to escape into a different time. I even caught him in the basement right after this house was built. We had a pretty brutal fight before he escaped to a different time. I hit him over the head with a wine bottle just before he jumped. I had to stay behind and clean up the blood he left so the family wouldn't find it."

"So," Jake began warily. "You said that he killed Janet. Why would he do that?"

"Because he thought that if he killed her, he would prevent me from being born and that would stop me from chasing him through time."

Jake's head was spinning. His mind was having a difficult time grasping this new reality. Could this all be an elaborate hoax? The house had literally changed within minutes to a newer version.

Nobody could pull that off unless what Zander was telling him was true. Jake suddenly realized that he had been staring at the floor, lost in his thoughts when Zander's voice brought him out of his trance.

"Derek thought that by killing Janet, I wouldn't be born, and he would avoid prosecution for his crimes. But when I found him after that, he realized that he had made a mistake. Janet was not my ancestor. I came from Thomas' second wife, Bridget."

"So, I guess that means Thomas and Bridget are going to have kids together, huh?"

"Yes," Zander replied. "And if I'm going to preserve my own life, I need to keep her alive."

"Okay, so what's the plan? Why are you telling *me* this instead of Thomas?"

"Well, in answer to your first question, I don't have a specific plan yet. And to answer your second question, I can't get Thomas to come to the house. I tried to get him to come over when I called him to rent the place. As you can see, I don't really need to rent it. I was trying to get Thomas to come here so that I could time jump with him and prove who I was. Since I couldn't get him here, I had to try you."

"So, you didn't meet up with him to get a key?"

"We've only spoken on the phone. When I contacted him to rent the place, he told me there was a key hidden under a planter on the front porch."

Jake stared at Zander in amazement. Here was a time traveler standing in front of him; a man who had supposedly come from the future to prevent his ancestor from being murdered. But why did a man who could travel through time need his help?

"So, if you can travel through time," Jake asked. "Why couldn't you change the past and prevent Janet from being murdered?

"Actually, I have saved her a couple of times. Derek killed her the first time in her sleep; bludgeoned her to death. Thomas actually went to prison for that one. Then he broke into the house and stabbed her in the kitchen. After going back in time to change that, I happened to come across some old news archives and found that Janet would have died of cancer. I realized that if she were kept alive, I would not exist, so when Derek killed her this last time, I didn't try to stop it, which, in a way, is good because altering the past tends to create time fragments."

"So, you've traveled back in time with no plan but somehow, you're going to prevent another murder from happening, so you won't cease to exist?"

"I'm actually trying to prevent two murders, Jake. I need to prevent Derek from killing Bridget and I also want to save the person he killed in the future."

"So, what happens next?" Jake asked with a shrug.

"I need you to talk to Thomas. He needs to know what's happening but since he won't come to the house it's going to be a little difficult to get him to believe that people have traveled back in time and one of them is planning to kill his future wife."

"And how are we supposed to prevent that from happening?"

Zander paused. "I don't know. We're going to have to figure that out."

Suddenly, Jake remembered the man at the cemetery. He had only seen him from a distance so he couldn't really make out what he looked like. "Were you at Janet's funeral?" he asked.

"Yes, I was, and I know that you saw me there. I was trying to keep out of sight, hoping that Derek would show up so I could grab him, but I never saw him there."

"Why did you wait a year after Janet's death to make contact with me?" Jake demanded.

Zander looked at him for a moment before responding. "It's complicated. It would have been better if I had not contacted you at all, but Derek knows that he killed the wrong woman, and he's going to go after Bridget."

"Why didn't he just kill Thomas, since he knows for sure that he is your ancestor?"

"Oh, he has killed Thomas," Zander replied. "Several times."

Jake threw up his hands and said, "Of course he has."

"Yeah, but it was after Bridget was pregnant, so it didn't really count. He messed up his time jump and got here at the wrong time. I've had to go back and change the past a few times. But as I said, that tends to leave some fragments in the space-time continuum."

"Fragments?" Jake asked. "What kind of fragments?"

"Well, ones like you experienced the other day when you were over here working on the house. You know when you ran into the original owners of the house – George Holman and his family."

Jake felt a sudden shock. "That was the family who built the house?" he asked.

"Yes," Zander replied. "That little girl you saw was their daughter, Annie."

Jake's mind was racing. "So why could I see them, but they couldn't see me?"

"Because they were a time fragment," Zander answered. "You were really in the house, but they were a left over from Derek and me jumping in and out of their time."

Jake stood motionless, staring at Zander with his mouth open. It was a lot to process, and he felt like his brain might melt.

Zander continued his explanation of time fragments. "Another case of time fragments are the scars that the coroner found on Janet's body this last time. Those scars were from other times Derek got to her. It's weird how time fragments manifest themselves."

"Yeah, weird," Jake stammered.

"But I don't yet know what the long-term consequences of changing past events will be," Zander said, almost talking to himself. "So, I'm hoping to avoid that in the future. Hopefully, the ripples we're creating in the fabric of time will iron themselves out once I catch Derek and take him back to our time for trial. Of course, killing him is also an option."

Jake's eyes widened. "Killing him?" he asked incredulously.

"Yes, killing him would probably be the cleanest option all the way around. It will leave some fragments in the space-time continuum but then we would be done with the whole thing."

Jake thought things over while keeping an eye on Zander. He was amazed at how cavalier Zander was about killing someone. He wasn't sure he could trust this man from the future. Nor was he convinced that Zander really was from the future or that any of his outlandish story was true. Suddenly, he had a bone chilling thought. 'What if Zander was really the bad guy?'

"Look," Jake said. "I'm not going to kill anybody, so if that's what you want me to help you do, then forget it. And how do I know that you're not really the bad guy?"

"First," Zander replied. "I'm not asking you to kill anybody. And second, you're right. There's no way for you to know whether I'm the good guy or the bad guy. At least not while we're standing here doing nothing."

"So, what do you want me to do?" Jake asked.

"I need you to get Thomas to come over here so I can talk to him."

"You want me to get him over here right now?" Jake asked defiantly.

"Yes," Zander chuckled as though Jake should have known that.

Jake pulled out his phone and dialed Thomas.

"Hey Jake, what's up?" came the voice on the other end.

"Uh, Thomas," Jake began hesitantly. "There's kind of a situation here at the old house you need to deal with. Could you please come over? I'm here right now with your renter."

After a moment of silence, Thomas responded, "I told you I wasn't ever going back to that house, Jake. I just can't."

"I know it's tough, Thomas, but I really need you to come over here. I'll meet you outside, okay?"

"Okay," Thomas said reluctantly, "I'll be there in 10 minutes."

Jake put his phone back in his pocket and turned to Zander. "So, just how do you time travel in this house?" he asked.

"Let me show you," Zander said with a hint of pride in his voice. "The time module is in the basement."

"So that's what's in the cabinet down there?" Jake asked as they made their way to the basement stairs. Zander seemed to ignore the question as they descended the stairs and walked across the room to the large cabinet. He opened the doors to reveal the strange looking apparatus with two bars that looked like handlebars on a bike and some dials in the middle.

"Now Jake, you have to promise me that you won't mess with this thing," Zander said sternly.

"Why would I?" Jake shrugged. "The last thing I want to do is create some time fragments."

Zander smiled. "No, we don't need any more of those."

"So, how does it work?" Jake asked.

Zander turned and looked him in the eye. "I'm not going to show you that, Jake. You're much safer not knowing. Besides, once were done with the mission, I'll take the device back to my time and you won't have to worry about it anymore. In fact, you might not have any memory of me at all."

"A mission," Jake snickered. "Is that what you're on? A mission?"

"Yes," Zander said seriously. "I'm on a mission to catch a killer and save the lives of you and your family."

"Yeah," Jake replied scornfully. "But not Janet, right?"

Zander sighed. "Jake, I told you that Janet would have died anyway. I know that's not what you want to hear, but it's the truth."

"So, all these strange things that have been happening in the house are because of this machine, right?" Jake asked. "There aren't really ghosts haunting this place are there?"

"That's right," Zander said. "Thomas and Janet may have been hearing time fragments, but they also may have heard either me or Derek in the house. They may have even seen time fragments of people who lived in this house in the past, just like you did. Who knows, they may have encountered future residents too."

Their conversation was interrupted by the sound of a car horn honking angrily outside. They rushed up the stairs and out the front door to find Thomas standing beside his car. "I thought you were going to meet me outside," he said angrily.

"Sorry, Thomas," Jake said, "Zander and I were talking, and I got distracted. We should've been waiting out here for you."

Zander walked toward Thomas and extended his hand. "Thomas, it's so nice to meet you. I'm Zander Knox."

"Yeah, I kind of figured that," Thomas said coldly.

Zander left his hand up for Thomas to shake, but Thomas didn't extend his own hand. He just stood with his back against his car as if he would jump into the driver's seat and race away at any minute. Finally, Zander lowered his hand.

"Well, uh, Thomas," Zander said nervously. "There's something I need you to see inside. Would you please come with me?"

"No," Thomas said firmly. "I said that I'm never going back into that house, and I meant it. If you want your rent money back, you can have it but I'm not going in that house. Not now, not ever."

Zander paused and looked at Jake.

"Look, Thomas," Jake began carefully. "I've been here talking with Zander for a while and if he's really who he says he is and the things he's been telling me are true, then we need to take him seriously."

Thomas began breathing heavy. "I can't go in that house, Jake. You know that!"

"Okay, let's just talk this through for a minute," Jake said, "Zander, can you talk to him out here?"

"It would be better to demonstrate things inside, but I'll give it a try if that's our only option."

"It is," Thomas said, resolutely.

"Okay," Zander said with a sigh. "What I'm going to tell you is going to be hard to believe, but if you want proof, we'll need to go inside the house, alright?"

Thomas didn't respond or move from his defensive position. He just looked steadfastly at Zander.

"I'm," Zander began cautiously, "from the future. I came to this time because there is a man intent on harming you and your family. I need your help to stop him."

"Somebody wants to hurt my family?" Thomas said glumly. "Somebody has already hurt my family."

"Yes, I know," Zander said softly. "His name is Derek Killian."

Thomas' demeanor suddenly changed. "Derek Killian?" he snapped. "No way! Derek is a nice guy."

Zander and Jake stood in stunned silence. Zander cocked his head, "You know Derek Killian? How?" he asked.

"He's a private investigator I hired to find out what or who really killed Janet."

'Could there be another Derek Killian?' Zander thought to himself. 'Or is this the man I've been tracking through time?'

Thomas' eyes seemed to glaze over as they teared up. Turning to Jake, he asked, "Why are you doing this?"

Zander answered, "Thomas, I'm not just trying to save your life, I'm trying to save my own. I am your descendant."

Thomas eyed Zander with contempt. "You're crazy," he hissed. "This house is crazy; this is all crazy! Maybe if this house wasn't here, this would all go away."

Thomas reached into his car and pulled out a gasoline-filled jar with a rag stuck through the lid. Before Zander or Jake could respond, Thomas ran toward the house as he lit the rag and threw the jar through the open doorway. The old wooden house went up in flames immediately. Zander ran toward the house. Jake grabbed his arm, trying to stop him.

"Zander, stop," he yelled. "It's too dangerous."

"I've got to get to the time module, or I'll be trapped here," Zander said, breaking away from Jake's grasp. He ran through the doorway and disappeared into the house. Jake ran after him. He didn't really think about it, he was just following his instincts to try and save Zander.

The house was already thick with smoke. Jake ran to the basement stairs and called Zander's name. No answer. He ran down the stairs and into the basement. Zander wasn't there. The time module was gone. Confused, he made his way back up the stairs. The smoke made his eyes water, making it difficult to see. He could hear Thomas outside yelling his name. He crouched down low to try to avoid the smoke but was soon overcome. He flopped down onto the floor and passed out.

Chapter Eight

Time Fragments

Jake's alarm went off at 5:30 A.M. as usual. He punched the button on top of his clock to turn it off and rolled onto his back. He stared at the ceiling while he tried to remember what day it was and why his mind was so blank. He took a deep breath and coughed. His lungs felt like they were burning. Suddenly, he remembered the events of the previous day and lurched out of bed. 'Oh my gosh,' he thought to himself, 'Thomas burned down the house.'

He sat on the edge of the bed while he tried to gather his thoughts, which seemed to be jumbled up and muddled. He wondered if it was a dream. No, the memory was much too vivid to be a dream. He walked into the bathroom where Mia was getting ready for the day.

"Are you okay?" she asked, noticing the odd look on his face in the mirror.

"I realize that this is a weird question to ask, but do you remember going over to Thomas' old house with me yesterday?"

She stopped brushing her cheeks and turned to look at him. "No," she said hesitantly, "I didn't go to the old house yesterday. Why, what's going on?"

Jake was silent while he tried to collect his thoughts. Finally, he said, "Nothing, I just had this crazy dream that Thomas burned the house down. It seemed so real."

Jake was quieter than usual as he ate breakfast. Mia noticed and asked again if he was okay.

"Yeah, I'm fine," Jake replied. "I'm just feeling a little weird today. I don't know why."

After breakfast, Jake climbed into his truck and pulled out of the driveway. As he rounded the corner, he expected to see nothing but burned rubble where the house on the corner sat, but to his surprise, the house was still standing, as if nothing had happened to it. An odd feeling settled over him. He clearly remembered the events of the previous day: seeing Thomas' kids playing outside, Janet alive again, meeting Zander, and Thomas burning the house down. What he did not remember was how he got out of the house and back home. His last memory was being overcome with smoke just before he passed out.

He swung into the driveway of the old house, jumped out of his truck, and walked to the front door. He wasn't sure whether he should knock or just walk in. As he arrived at the door, however, Zander opened it.

"Good morning, Jake," he said. "Did you sleep well?"

"What happened?" Jake demanded. "Did Thomas really set this place on fire?"

"Yes, he did," Zander answered. "But he won't remember it."

"Then why do I remember it?" Jake demanded.

"Because you were in the house. You were part of the time jump I activated to put the house back after the fire started."

"I don't remember anything after the fire," Jake said. "How did I get home?"

"You went home on your own," Zander answered. "After you left, I jumped again to try to clean up some time fragments. That's probably why you don't remember going home. Mia won't have any memory of the fire because she was on a different timeline, but I was concerned that Thomas might have some lingering memory. Hopefully, I've taken care of that."

"I can't believe he tried to burn the place down," Jake said.

"Yeah," Zander said, thoughtfully. "I guess we're going to have to find another way to protect him and his fiancé."

"Are you sure that Derek the private investigator is the killer?"

"No," said Zander. "I'm going to need you to find out. I would do it, but if it is him, he will recognize me. I don't want him to know I'm here if he doesn't already."

"How am I supposed to find out?" Jake asked. "I don't know what he looks like."

Zander produced a strange, futuristic looking mobile device and waved his hand across it. Then he turned it and showed Jake a photo of a man with short dark hair and a well-trimmed beard.

"This is Derek Killian," Zander said, as Jake studied the electronic image.

"Can you transfer that to my cell phone?" Jake asked.

"I don't know. The technology is more than a hundred years apart. Just take a picture of my screen with your phone."

Jake pulled out his phone and snapped a picture. He shoved his phone back into his pocket and asked, "Okay, what do we do now?"

"Go visit Thomas at his office. See if you can get him to introduce you to the investigator."

"That's easy enough. I'll head over there on my way to the construction site."

Jake drove to Thomas' office and parked his truck. He walked into the reception area and asked for Thomas.

"He didn't come in today," the receptionist said. "Looks like he called in sick."

Jake thanked her and walked out of the office. He was concerned about his brother, so he called him as he walked to his truck. Thomas didn't answer. As Jake approached his truck, he noticed a dark-haired man leaning up against it. As he came closer, he recognized Derek Killian from the photo that Zander had shown him.

He stopped walking and pretended to look at something on his phone. He didn't know what to do. Was Derek waiting to kill him? Should he abandon his truck and run? He needed to think it through. He lifted the phone to his ear and pretended to talk while he considered his options. From a distance it would look like he stopped to answer a text or take a call. Finally, he decided he had to face Derek. He put his phone in his pocket and walked toward his truck. As he got closer, Derek called out to him, "Hey Jake, how's it going?"

Jake stopped about ten feet away. "Who are you?" he demanded.

"Oh, you know who I am, Jake. We need to talk!"

Jake maintained his distance. "Yeah, I do know who you are. You're a killer!"

"I thought Zander would tell you that," Derek scoffed. "It's unfortunate that he got to you first. I'll bet he also told you that he's the one who invented the time machine."

"Well, yeah," Jake said cautiously. "Are you saying he's been lying to me?"

Derek smiled. "Yeah, that's what I'm saying, Jake. Everything Zander told you is a lie. He's not chasing me through time, I'm chasing him. And Zander didn't invent the time machine, he stole it. I'm a cop from the future and I was sent after him. He's a dangerous con man and I've got to stop him from causing any more problems."

"What problems is he causing?" Jake asked.

"You're not the first person he's tried to con, Jake. I've tracked him through time and watched him gain people's confidence so that he can take advantage of them. He usually starts by causing some traumatic event to get them emotionally vulnerable, sound familiar?"

"Yeah, but that doesn't fit in my case."

"Of course, it does," Derek said with a hint of irritation. "He killed your sister-in-law, Jake."

"But that scenario only fits if he was trying to get to Thomas," Jake argued.

"That's exactly what he's trying to do," Derek hissed, impatiently. "But his usual tactics haven't been working so now he's trying to get to Thomas through you."

Derek's story was beginning to make sense, and it shook Jake up. What if Derek's story was true? What if he had been trusting the wrong man? How was he going to figure out which one of them was telling the truth? He decided to push for more information.

"What about the murder that happens in the future?" Jake asked, hoping to trip Derek up.

"What murder?" Derek asked.

"Zander said that you killed somebody in the future and escaped using the time module. How do you explain that?"

"Wow," Derek said. "I haven't heard that one yet. He must be adding to the story as he goes."

"So, you're saying there was no murder in the future?" Jake asked, suspiciously.

"Not that I know of," Derek said calmy. "Zander attacked the scientist who invented the machine, but he didn't die."

"Let's suppose for a minute that I believe you," Jake said. "What do we do now?"

"I need you to help me catch Zander," Derek said. "I've got to take him by surprise."

Jake was confused. Maybe Derek really was telling the truth. If he wanted to kill Thomas or his fiancé, he would have had plenty of opportunities while posing as a private investigator.

On the other hand, if Zander was telling the truth and he took Derek to him, the result could be disastrous. If Derek was as mentally unstable as Zander claimed, he could really mess up things.

"I need to think this over," Jake said. "I'm going to check on Thomas before I do anything else."

"Thomas is fine," Derek said.

Suddenly, Derek started to twitch and jerk as if he was an electronic image that was glitching. His image blinked in and out momentarily then disappeared completely. Jake stared in the direction Derek had been standing in disbelief. He looked around to see if anybody else had seen what just happened. There was nobody else in sight. Jake walked cautiously to his truck, worried that it was a clever trick, and that Derek would reappear suddenly and grab him. When he got to the door of his truck, he quickly unlocked it and jumped into the driver's seat. He slammed the door shut and locked it.

He looked around then quickly drove out of the parking lot and out onto the road. He drove to Thomas' house and found his car parked in front. Worried that something might have happened to him, he rushed to the door and rang the doorbell. He was relieved when Thomas opened the door.

"Oh, hey Jake, what's up?" Thomas said when he saw his brother standing at the door.

"I went by your office to talk to you, and they said that you called in sick. I tried to call but you didn't answer your phone, so I thought I better come by to make sure you're alright."

"Yeah, I'm fine," Thomas answered. "I just woke up this morning with this weird cough. I don't know if it's bad enough to go to the doctor but it kind of hurts to breathe."

Jake immediately thought of the events of the night before. Thomas set the house on fire but as far as Jake knew, he never went inside. Considering his brother's delicate emotions regarding the house, he decided to approach the subject carefully.

"What do you think caused it?" Jake asked.

"I don't know," Thomas said. "But the weirdest thing happened. Last night I dreamed that the house on the corner caught on fire. I was standing in front, watching it burn. This morning I woke up with this cough and I swear I could smell smoke. It's amazing how powerful our imagination is."

"Wow," Jake said, acting surprised. "Why do you think you had that dream?"

"I don't know, bro," Thomas answered. "Dreams are weird."

"Oh, hey, by the way," Jake said, changing the subject. "I met your private investigator today."

"Oh, yeah?" Thomas asked. "What's he like?"

"What, you haven't met him?"

"No, I've only talked to him on the phone."

"How did you find him?" Jake asked, surprised at Thomas' answer.

"He called me," Thomas replied. "He said that he was at the police station the other day when you and I were there being interrogated. He heard us talking in the lobby when we were leaving, and he thought he could help me out, so he got my phone number and called me."

"What's he going to do for you?" Jake asked.

"Well, he said that he had information that could clear me of the charges the police were trying to pin on me. He wanted to meet with me and Bridget, but we haven't come up with a time that works yet, so…"

"Why would Bridget need to be there?"

"I don't know, but he was pretty insistent that she needed to be there when we meet."

Thomas' explanation shed new light on Derek. It appeared that he was just looking for a way to get to Bridget. It was hard to know who to trust. Derek's story was compelling but so was Zander's. Jake worried about trusting the wrong person and what consequences it would bring.

Jake left Thomas' house and went to his job site, but he found that he was unable to concentrate on his work. His conversation with Derek had cast doubt on the situation and he realized that he didn't really know who to trust. If Derek had been able to meet with Thomas and nothing had happened, he might have found his story more plausible. But since he had not had the opportunity, Jake couldn't rule out the possibility that Zander was the good guy and Derek was just what Zander said he was: a time-traveling murderer.

His thoughts turned to his conversation with Derek. What caused Derek to suddenly disappear? The way he started glitching before he disappeared made Jake wonder if he was really just a futuristic holographic transmission that was disrupted, and not an actual person.

Since he wasn't getting any work done, Jake decided to go by the police station and ask for more information on Janet's autopsy. Maybe talking to the police might help him figure out who he could trust - if anybody. The detective who previously interrogated Jake invited him into his office. Jake asked if there were more details from the autopsy that the detective could share.

"Actually, there is one detail I didn't share with you," the detective said in response to Jake's request. "But we don't know if it has any relevance to the case."

Jake waited for the detective to share the information, but he just sat on the other side of his desk and stared at Jake. Finally, Jake broke the silence. "Well, what is it? What else did they find?

"Mrs. Holman had a malignant brain tumor," the officer replied.

Jake tipped his head back and looked at the ceiling. 'Wow,' he thought to himself. 'Zander was right.'

"There's a theory we're working on in this case," the detective continued. "And that is that your brother knew his wife was dying from a brain tumor, so he decided to spare her the pain and suffering she would have inevitably gone through."

Jake found the detective's statement offensive. He sat forward in his chair and leaned across the desk, pointing his finger at the man. "That's ridiculous and you know it!" he said. Without another word, he got up and walked out of the office.

He left the police station and drove to the house on the corner to talk to Zander. He was beginning to trust Zander more, but he was still cautious. He worried that both time travelers might be psychopaths and everything they said was a lie. Even more concerning was the thought that they might be working together.

When Zander came to the door, Jake immediately noticed something was wrong. Zander looked pale and he was holding his left arm like it was in a sling. He seemed to be in a lot of pain. He had scrapes and bruises on his face and forehead.

"What happened to you?" Jake demanded when he saw Zander.

"Well, let's just say that I ended Derek's career as a private investigator. I'm afraid there's going to be another time fragment floating out there."

"Is he dead?" Jake asked accusingly. "Did you kill him?"

"No," Zander replied. "But I sure tried to."

Jake looked at Zander for a moment before demanding answers. "So, what exactly happened?" he asked.

"Well," Zander started coyly. "I wanted to see what happened at the police station when you and Thomas were there being questioned about the murder, so I jumped back to that time to check it out. I walked into the police station and found Derek there, so I attacked him in the lobby. As you might imagine, the police broke it up and arrested both of us. Derek is still there. I imagine he's going to have a hard time getting out."

"How did you get out?" Jake asked.

"I knew that things might not quite go right so I programmed the time module for an automatic jump. I would have liked to see the look on my cellmates' faces when I disappeared," he said with a smirk on his face.

"You can time travel from the jail?" Jake asked. "I thought you had to be in the house."

"Technically you do, but I've figured out how to set the machine to grab me from outside the house."

"So, what, it like sucks you back to the house?"

"Something like that," Zander said, growing impatient.

"That's kind of funny to visualize," Jake snickered. "Like the house is this giant vacuum sucking you through the air…"

"By the way, how did it go with Thomas?" Zander blurted, changing the subject.

"Oh, well, I talked to Derek today."

"No kidding?"

"Yeah," Jake said. "And while was talking to him, he disappeared."

Zander chuckled, "That would be because I got him thrown in jail and altered his future on that timeline. When that happened, he was in jail instead of with you. So anyway, what happened? Tell me all about it."

"Well, I went to Thomas' office like you asked and found out that Thomas called in sick. When I walked back to my truck, Derek was waiting for me."

"Oh really?" Zander said, raising his eyebrows. He waited for Jake to continue but Jake remained silent. Finally, he asked, "So, what happened? What did he say?"

"He said that you've been lying to me," Jake said with a hint of accusation in his voice. "He said you didn't invent the time machine; you just stole it. He claims that he's a cop and he's the one chasing you through time."

"Ah," Zander said. "So, he's playing that game." He studied Jake momentarily before continuing. "And what do think, Jake? Do you believe him?"

"How am I supposed to know which one of you is telling the truth, or if you're both just playing a game? Because, honestly, all of this feels like a game to me."

Zander sighed, "I can see how you would feel that way. I am sorry I brought you into this. The important thing is that you protect your family, and especially Thomas' fiancé. Derek will try to kill her at the wedding."

"How do you know that?" Jake asked with a hint of suspicion in his voice.

Zander chuckled, "Because in my time, it's already happened, and I stopped it. I just couldn't catch Derek."

"You told me you came here without a plan," Jake said accusingly.

"I don't have a plan," Zander replied. "But I never said that I don't know when Derek is going to try to kill Bridget."

"Yeah, but you've been acting like you have no idea, and now you say you know when and where it will happen," Jake said, heatedly.

"I'm sorry," Zander said. "If you remember, I was trying to get to Thomas. If that would have worked out, I may not have needed your help, but clearly Thomas can't deal with any of this, so I'm going with plan B."

"What's plan B?" Jake asked.

"You are plan B."

"What am I supposed to do?"

"I don't know yet," Zander replied. "I'll let you know when I figure it out."

The two men eyed each other for a moment in silence.

"By the way," Jake said, breaking the silence, "Thomas seems to have one of those time fragments you've talked about. I stopped by his house to check on him and he told me that he dreamed last night that the house burned down. This morning he woke up with a bad cough."

"Oh, well, he'll be alright," Zander said with some hesitation. "I think."

"So how is it supposed to go down at the wedding?" Jake asked, "Is Derek going to show up with some kind of futuristic ray gun and vaporize her at the alter?"

Zander laughed, "What makes you think we have ray guns in the future? In your time guns were invented 200 years ago and while the guns may have improved, you're still shooting bullets. I assure you they're still using bullets in my time as well."

Jake's mind was heavy with doubt as he drove around the corner to his home. While the evidence indicated that Zander was more trustworthy than Derek, he was still concerned that there was more going on than either time traveler was letting on. What he did know was that his family was in danger, and he was determined to protect his wife and his brother's family from harm, regardless of the cost.

Chapter Nine

Time Travel Experiments 150 years in the future

Zander Knox was confident his experiment would work. His research had proven his theory that time travel was possible using DNA as the basis for jumping from one time to another. Like theoretical experiments of the past in which scientists had sent particles back in time by a few seconds, Zander believed that DNA could provide an extension to the time frame that particles could travel. And he believed that he could move a person through time as long as there was a DNA link to the destination. The house on the corner had been in his family for more than 250 years. DNA from his ancestors would provide a long range for his experiments.

Zander's team consisted of himself and two colleagues: Roger Jacobs and Connor Firth. Time travel was little more than theory when the team began working on their project as post-graduate students. Zander had been living in the house but moved into an apartment when they began using it for their experiments.

After years of theorizing, the team had built a time module in the basement that they tested by sending Zander back in time. It was noon on the day they were ready to test the machine. Zander set the controls to take him back to 11:00 A.M. The test was successful except for an unexpected error. Zander had been in the room at 11:00. When he sent himself back to that time, his future self collided with his past self and bounced his future self forward to noon. To his colleagues in the room, it was as if he never left. But Zander knew what had happened and he knew that the machine worked. The test also proved that two versions of himself could not occupy the same place in time.

For his next experiment he traveled back to the beginning of the day and was waiting in the entryway when his team showed up for work. He knew that they would not expect him to be there and was looking forward to surprising them when they arrived.

His two colleagues arrived right on time and were chatting as they walked toward the front door. "No," Roger said as he walked through the door. "Zander's never here this early."

Zander was notorious for coming to work late and Roger and Connor were making bets on what time he would show up.

Time traveling Zander couldn't restrain himself from joining their conversation about his habitual tardiness. "What time do you think I'll get here?" he asked in amusement.

Roger looked up and saw Zander standing in the entryway. "What, did you stay here all night?" he asked.

"No," Zander answered, "I'm time traveling. I came here from this afternoon."

"No way!" Roger said in disbelief.

"Are you serious?" Connor said, almost tripping as he walked through the door into the entryway.

"I'm dead serious," Zander said with a big grin. "But I was here earlier than usual this morning. Look behind you."

Roger and Connor turned and looked through the open front door and saw Zander walking up the sidewalk. He strolled up to the front door and walked into the house. When he looked up and saw himself standing in the entryway with his colleagues, a wry smile crossed his face. Then everything changed. Suddenly, Zander found himself racing through time back to the afternoon of the same day when he left. He let go of the handlebars of the time module and turned around. Roger and Connor were standing behind him with their mouths open.

"You guys okay?" Zander asked

"You totally disappeared for a few seconds, then came back," Connor said.

"Yeah, that was really creepy," Roger observed. "What happened?"

Zander looked at his colleagues as he contemplated their success. He smiled. "It worked, guys," he said, "I traveled back to this morning just before you showed up for work."

"No way," Connor said. "Really?"

"Yes," Zander replied. He told them about the brief encounter he had with them during his time jump and how he was suddenly whisked back to the time he left when he saw himself walk through the door.

"Wait a minute," Roger said, suddenly. "Why don't I remember this happening? If you time jumped back to this morning, I should remember it now, right?"

"Wow, I don't remember it either," Connor said.

Zander thought for a minute. "I don't know, maybe it's because you're on a different timeline. Maybe I remember it because I am in both timelines."

Roger and Connor stared at him blankly.

"I don't know, guys, it's just a theory," Zander continued. "I'll have to make more jumps to figure it out."

"So, what's next?" Connor asked.

"Well, let's call it a day for now and figure out our next step tomorrow," Zander said. "You guys go ahead and go home. I'm going to make a few notes about what we did today."

"Hey, maybe you should go back about 30 years and see yourself as a kid," Roger suggested.

"You know, that's not a bad idea," Zander said after thinking it over. "Then we would have something to compare with today's jump."

The three of them climbed the stairs out of the basement and Roger and Connor left. Zander was gathering some things up from the room he used for an office when he heard a noise in the kitchen. The sun had set, and the house was dark except for the light in Zander's office. He walked toward the kitchen, a little nervous that someone might be in the house. He switched on the kitchen light and looked around. Nobody was there. As he turned off the light and began to walk back to his office, he heard a voice from the dining room behind him.

"Don't you have anything to eat around here?"

Startled, Zander whirled around to see who was talking to him. In the dim light, he saw somebody sitting at the dining room table. He flipped the lights on to see a tall, slender but muscular man with short black hair and a well-trimmed beard.

"Hi Zander," the man said. "Long time no see."

"Do I know you?" Zander asked suspiciously.

"Yeah, you do," the dark-haired man said, "I used to live in this house with you. I mean it was a long time ago, but – "

"Derek?" Zander asked, "Are you Derek Killian?"

"See, I knew it would come back to you," Derek said slyly.

"I thought you were in prison," Zander stated.

"I was," Derek replied. "Just got out as a matter of fact." He stood up and walked toward Zander. "Good behavior and all, you know?"

Zander backed away as Derek came toward him. "What are you doing here?" he asked suspiciously.

"Well, I just got out of prison, and didn't have any place to go, so I came here," Derek said.

He paused and looked at Zander as if he was expecting him to offer help, but Zander just stood still, gazing at him in disbelief.

"Oh, come on, Zander. I thought maybe I could crash here for a while, just until I get things together."

"No," Zander replied quickly. "You can't stay here. This is a research facility. You're going to have to find someplace else to go."

"A research facility?" Derek said, mockingly. "It sure looks like a house to me."

"You can't stay here, Derek," Zander said emphatically."

Derek thought for a moment. "So, what are you researching?" he asked, trying to keep the conversation going.

"You can't stay here, Derek," Zander repeated. "You need to leave."

Derek stood motionless. He had been counting on staying with Zander while he got back on his feet, but that hope was quickly fading.

"Okay," Derek finally said. "I'm sorry I bothered you."

Derek walked out the door and into the night. Zander breathed a sigh of relief as he watched him walk down the street. He closed the door and locked it. Then he checked the other doors to make sure the house was secure before going home for the night. He was concerned that Derek would come back while he was gone and try to sneak back into the house to sleep. He wondered if he was being too hard on him, but there was too much at stake. He couldn't risk a criminal like Derek learning about the time travel project.

Derek had come to live with Zander's family when he was about 12 years old. He had a troubled childhood and had worn out his welcome in at least a half dozen foster homes. His parents were career criminals and never had any interest in Derek. He became a ward of the state when he was just six years old.

Zander wondered if he should have had more compassion for Derek, but he had made life difficult for Zander when he lived with his family. Zander's possessions would turn up missing and would often be found in Derek's bedroom. Some missing items were never found, and Zander suspected that he either sold them or traded them for drugs. Derek eventually went to prison for possession of stolen property and selling drugs.

The next morning, when Zander arrived for work, he found his research facility surrounded by police vehicles. He quickly ran up to the front door where he was intercepted by a police officer.

"You can't go in there, sir," the officer said as he held up his hand.

"What's going on? What happened?" Zander asked impatiently.

"There's been a murder," the officer said.

"Oh my," Zander said. "This is my house. You can't keep me out. I've got to find out what happened."

Deep down, Zander knew that Derek must be involved. He suspected that the murder victim must be one or both of his research assistants. His mind was racing, and panic was building inside of him.

A police detective came to the door. "Are you Zander?" he asked authoritatively.

"Yes," Zander answered.

"Your research team said you were usually late," the detective said. "Come in!"

"What's going on?" Zander asked as he walked through the door.

"Well, apparently, your guys showed up this morning and found a murder victim in the basement. We got a call about an hour ago from Roger Jacobs reporting it."

The detective led him down to the basement where Roger and Connor rushed across the room to greet him. They were visibly shaken, but he was relieved to see that they were okay. Across the room near the time machine cabinet laid the body of the victim, covered with a sheet.

"What happened?" Zander asked.

Roger and Connor looked at each other as if they were silently trying to determine who was going to tell the story.

Connor began, "We showed up this morning and…"

"Actually, I got here first," Roger interrupted. "I was in the kitchen making coffee when Connor got here."

"Right," Connor agreed. "Then we went downstairs and found the body."

"Yeah," Roger said nervously. "I'm still freaked out."

"Who is it? Who's the victim?" Zander asked.

"We were hoping you could tell us," the detective said. "These two guys say they've never seen him before."

Zander's heart sank. He suspected Derek was under the sheet, but he couldn't figure out what might have killed him. He followed the detective across the room where he pulled the sheet back. Zander braced himself as he prepared to look at the corpse. To his surprise, it wasn't Derek. The body under the sheet was a stranger.

"Do you recognize him?" the detective asked.

Zander shook his head. "No," he answered, "I've never seen this man before."

"So, no idea why he'd be here?" the detective asked.

"No," Zander replied.

"What do you guys do here?" the detective asked. "What's this thing in the cabinet?" he asked pointing to the time module.

"Scientific research," Zander answered curtly.

"What kind of scientific research?" the detective pressed.

Zander and his assistants were at a loss to answer. They didn't want anybody to know the nature of their research, but they had no official reason to keep it a secret. Finally, Roger knew what to say.

"Uh, our research is classified. We're not allowed to discuss it."

The detective sighed. "Well, we have a dead body down here and I need to know how he died and who or what killed him. It looks like he was operating this machine," the detective said, pointing to the time module. "And somebody came up behind him and hit him in the head with a blunt object. Any idea why somebody would do that?"

Roger and Connor looked at Zander, expecting him to take the lead. Zander knew that Derek must be involved but he had no idea who the victim was or why he was in the basement of the research facility.

"I don't know who this man is or why he's in my research facility," Zander said. "But I know that a man named, Derek Killian, must be involved."

Zander went on to explain how Derek had been there the night before, that he had lived there as a foster child and how he had eventually gone to prison.

"Derek said that he had just gotten out of prison and wanted a place to stay," Zander told the detective. "Because of past experience with him, I told him he couldn't stay here."

"Okay," the detective said after hearing the story. "What motive would Killian have for killing the John Doe?"

"I have no idea," Zander said. Then he had a thought. "Did you guys check the cameras?" he asked, turning to Roger and Connor.

"You guys have cameras down here?" the detective asked.

"We have them throughout the building," Zander said. "We can look at the footage in my office upstairs."

Zander led the group up to his office. He turned on his computer and punched in the code for the camera feed, but it wouldn't come up.

"I think I can access it on my mobile," Connor said, pulling out his phone. He pulled up the security camera app and programmed in the time and date he wanted to see. "Trouble is," he said as he looked at his phone. "We don't know what time this happened."

"The camera should have an auto-start when it senses motion," Roger said as he leaned in to view the screen on the mobile device.

"I searched that feature, but it apparently didn't detect any motion last night. There's nothing here."

Without thinking, Connor backed the video feed up to the day before when Zander time jumped for the first time. It showed him standing at the time module controls for a moment before suddenly disappearing. A few seconds later he reappeared. The detective was trying to crowd in close enough to view the feed and caught the time jump.

"Looks like there's a bit of a glitch in your feed," he said, not understanding what he was seeing. "You glitched out for a few seconds, then came back. It looks like your system is a little unreliable."

Fortunately, the detective didn't notice that Roger and Connor stayed in full view while Zander disappeared during the time jump. Connor jumped the video forward and selected the feed from the dining room and kitchen that showed Zander talking to Derek the night before.

Zander pointed to the screen and said, "That's the man you're looking for. I don't know exactly what his involvement is in this murder, but he's definitely got to be involved."

While they were reviewing video, a couple of morgue technicians arrived with a gurney to take the body away for an autopsy. The detective directed them down to the basement. The two men wheeled their gurney toward the basement door, then bumped it down each step all the way to the basement. Soon one of them came back upstairs and asked where the body was.

"It's down in the basement against the far wall," the detective said. "You can't miss it."

"There's nothing down there," the morgue tech said. "At least there's no body."

The detective rushed down the stairs followed by Zander and his assistants. At the bottom of the stairs, they found the other mogue tech standing next to the empty gurney, but the victim's body was gone.

"What's going on?" the detective demanded, turning to Zander. "Who took the body out of here?"

Zander shrugged. "I have no idea."

"Maybe the other officers already took him upstairs," Roger suggested.

"That's not their job," the detective barked.

"Well, there's no way anybody could get it out of here without taking it upstairs," Connor said. "The window down here is too high to stuff a body through. If they tried taking it out the back, we would have seen them. They had to have taken the body out the front door, which means that one of your men would have seen them."

The detective shoved everybody out of his way and trudged up the stairs to confront the officers staged at the front of the house. The morgue technicians stayed in the basement waiting for further orders.

The detective stormed up to the officer at the front door. "Who took the body out of here?" he demanded of the confused officer.

"Nobody has brought the body out of the house sir," the officer replied with a hint of fear. "The morgue technicians just arrived and are downstairs with the body now."

"There is no body downstairs," the detective barked. "When the morgue techs went down to get it the body was gone. Somebody took it out of here and it had to come past you."

The officer swallowed hard. "Sir, nobody has taken the body out this door."

"Then we need to mobilize a search of the area," the detective barked. "Somebody got that body out of the house, and they can't be far away."

Soon a contingent of police officers arrived at the house, sirens blaring. While the detective was giving instructions to search the area, the morgue techs came out with a body on their gurney.

"Who's on the gurney?" the detective demanded.

"The John Doe we were sent to get," one of the techs said.

"Where did you find him?" the detective asked.

"In the basement."

"Who took him back down to the basement?" the detective demanded.

"I don't follow you, sir," the tech said. "He was in the basement when we got here. We just packed him up and brought him out."

"Something very strange is going on here," the detective muttered, shaking his head.

The body was loaded into a van and the morgue techs left. The detective went back in the house where Zander and his two assistants were waiting in the living room. The detective walked into the room and put his hands on his hips.

"I don't know what's going on here, but I'm going to get to the bottom of it," he said.

"I hope you do," Zander replied. "I really hope you can solve this murder."

"Are you taunting me?" the detective asked angrily.

"Not at all," Zander replied. "I sincerely want your help solving this crime."

The detective felt embarrassed and defeated. He didn't know what else to do other than to take the three researcher's contact information. He told them he would be in touch as he left the house.

After the authorities left, Zander, Roger and Connor sat at the dining room table discussing the recent events. Zander was concerned that Derek might have been watching them operate the time module and would try to use the machine for personal gain.

"Good thing he doesn't have the right DNA," Roger said.

"I'm afraid he does have the right DNA," Zander said. "I looked at his background last night. It turns out that we're distant relatives. He can trace his ancestors back to this house as well. Plus, he lived here for a while when we were kids. I'm guessing that must be how the body disappeared."

"Yeah, but it would be pretty risky," Roger continued. "Considering we just barely figured it out ourselves."

"Yes, but Derek is not afraid of risks," Zander said. "He generally acts before he thinks."

"The question I have is, 'how did he erase the video?'" Connor interjected.

"Good question," Zander said, suddenly realizing that they should examine the video footage more closely. They went back to Zander's office where he tried pulling the video up again. His access code still wasn't working.

"It seems that I've been locked out of my own system," Zander said as he typed on his keyboard. Finally, he tried an old code that let him access the video feed. He scrolled through it looking for clues about what happened the previous night. Scanning the outside cameras, they saw Derek walk up to the back door and open it with a key. Zander paused the video.

"He's got a key," he said. "How did he get a key?"

The video showed Derek enter the house and walk down into the basement. He walked up to the cabinet that contained the time module and opened the door. He reached in and grabbed the bars. Suddenly, he disappeared, and a body appeared on the floor.

All three men let out an audible gasp as they viewed the video.

"He must have time jumped," Zander exclaimed.

They scrolled back and forth, watching the scene over and over. It was impossible to know if Derek erased the video or erased some events by time jumping. As they debated the situation, they heard the voice of a child calling out. They stopped talking to listen.

"Mom?" they heard the young voice say. "Mom, please call me back. Something weird is happening at the house and I'm scared. Please call me back as soon as you can."

Then the boy began to sob. The men followed the sound up the stairs and into a bedroom. They found a boy about 10 years old, sitting on the floor with his head buried in his arms. Zander recognized the boy right away and gasped. He gently approached the boy. "Hey," he said softly. "Are you okay?"

The boy looked up and screamed when he saw three men standing in front of him.

"Who are you guys," he sobbed as he backed up closer to the wall. "Please don't hurt me. I don't know anything about treasure hidden in the house."

"We're not going to hurt you," Zander replied. "Why do you think we're here to harm you?"

"Yeah, kid," Connor said. "You're perfectly safe."

The boy looked back and forth at the three men as if he was sizing them up, trying to determine if they were telling the truth.

"So, you're not with that other man?" the boy asked.

"What other man?" Zander questioned.

"The dark-haired man with the beard. He showed up in my bedroom tonight. He had a knife. He asked me a bunch of weird questions about treasure hidden in the house. I got away from him and ran down to the basement and found this weird cabinet that wasn't there before. I tried to climb into the cabinet to hide from the man and the next thing I knew, he was gone, and the house was different. All our stuff was gone and then you guys showed up."

"We're not with the other guy," Zander said calmly. "You're safe.

"What's your name, little man?" Roger asked.

"Zander," the boy answered.

Suddenly both Roger and Connor realized what the older Zander already knew: This kid was ten-year-old Zander Knox.

"Holy crap," Connor said, "is this kid really…" he paused, weighing the effect his words would have on the boy. "How did this happen?" he asked.

The boy's eyes darted back and forth between the three men.

"Is this kid what?" he asked. "What were you going to say?"

The men looked at each other, wondering how to answer the question. Finally, older Zander sat down on the floor and scooted up next to his younger self.

"Zander, you know how you've always dreamed of time travel?"

"How do you know that?" young Zander asked.

"Because I'm you," old Zander replied. He waited for the boy to process the words.

"No way," the boy finally said.

"You know that machine in the basement?" older Zander asked.

"Yeah?" the boy answered.

"Well, that's a time machine."

The boy looked at him in disbelief.

"When you tried to hide in the cabinet in the basement," older Zander continued, "you activated the machine, and it brought you 40 years into the future."

"Really?" the boy squeaked.

"Really!" the older man confirmed, "You and I did it, Zander. We time traveled. I am you 40 years in the future."

"Wow," the boy whispered. He sat up and cleared his throat. "Then who is that guy that was trying to kill me?" he asked.

"His name is Derek Killian," Zander explained, "You haven't met him yet, but in a few years, you're going to meet him as a boy."

"But why is he trying to kill me?" young Zander asked.

"He's a criminal," older Zander said. "He killed a man in my time, and he doesn't want to get caught. Somehow, he figured out how the time module works and used it to escape. I think he came looking for you in the past. He must think that if he kills you, I won't exist and won't be able to catch him."

"But don't worry, kid," Roger piped in. "We won't let him get to you."

"So why can both of you be here since our earlier tests booted you back when you met yourself?" Connor asked.

"I've been asking myself the same question," Zander replied. "I don't have an answer right now, but my guess is that it has something to do with the fact that my DNA has changed somewhat over the last forty years."

"So, what's the plan, then?" Connor asked.

"I don't know," middle-aged Zander said, scratching his head. "I guess I'm going to have to go after Derek."

"What about the kid?" Roger asked.

"Let's keep him here with us for now," Zander replied. "We may need him to help us catch Derek."

Zander led his two colleagues and his younger self down to the basement. He was determined to find Derek and bring him back to face justice. He just didn't know where or when to look for him since he had the ability to travel through time.

"I know what time period you might find Derek in," young Zander offered.

The three scientists stopped their conversation and looked at the young boy.

"Okay," older Zander said, "What time period should I start with?"

"Derek said that the man who built this house had hidden some treasure in it. He said that the man had been a spy during the first world war, and he had stolen a bunch of stuff in Europe and smuggled it to the United States after the war. He said that he was here looking for it. My guess is that he went back to that time to look for it."

After hearing this, Zander realized that he had to travel back to the early 1900s. He didn't know exactly when the house was built or the name of the man who built it, but he knew that the man was his ancestor. He retreated to his office and logged into his computer to do some research. His search returned some interesting information about the home's original owner, George Holman.

Holman had been a British news correspondent stationed in the Netherlands in the early 1900s when he met a young German lady named, Greta. George and Greta began spending time together and soon fell in love. Greta was believed to have been a member of the German royal family but her royal lineage had never been traced.

When World War I broke out, George was recruited to be a spy for the British military. He was stationed in Rotterdam. He was sworn to secrecy and instructed not to tell anybody he was a spy, especially his German wife.

When the war ended in 1918, George was discharged from the British secret service and divulged his prior secret status to Greta. Whether or not George knew of his wife's royal status is unknown. It is believed that Greta didn't want her connection to the royal family to be publicly known for fear of retaliation for the atrocities committed by the German army during the war. George didn't feel like he could go back to England with a German wife, and Greta couldn't go back to Germany, so the couple decided the best course of action was to immigrate to the United States.

It was rumored that Greta had considerable wealth as a German royal and that they brought that with them when they immigrated to America. It is believed that George built a secret chamber in the basement of his home to hide a considerable amount of gold and silver as well as priceless jewelry and family heirlooms.

Armed with this information, Zander was ready to make his first significant jump. He was going back to 1920 when George Holman's house was new. Hopefully, he would find Derek Killian and bring him back for justice.

Zander programmed the time module for the jump and his fellow scientists wished him luck. He took hold of the handles and was suddenly whizzing back in time. He watched in amazement as the basement setting changed according to the time frame he was passing through. Soon he arrived in 1920.

The smell of fresh paint was an obvious clue that he had arrived when the house was new. He let go of the handles and closed the cabinet door. As he turned to sneak upstairs, he tripped over something on the floor. It was a body; the victim that Derek had murdered in the future. As he stood over the body, he heard people coming down the stairs. He knew he couldn't leave the body there for them to find so he wrestled it back to the time module and jumped into the future.

He arrived back in his time with the body just before the technicians came downstairs to transport it to the morgue. After staging the body where it was originally found, Zander time jumped back to 1920. This time he found Derek there.

Derek's eyes widened when he saw Zander appear in the basement. Zander immediately lunged at him, but Derek quickly turned and ran for the stairs. Zander caught him just before he made it to the top step.

"You're going to pay for the murder you committed," Zander said as he tried to gain control of Derek.

Derek was laying prone at the top of the stairs, straining to reach the doorknob while Zander held his feet, trying to drag him back down the stairs. Derek frantically tried to kick free of Zander's grasp, but Zander had such a tight grip that he couldn't move his feet. Finally, Derek twisted his upper body around and started punching Zander in the face.

"You're not taking me anywhere," he screamed. "I'll kill you too if you don't stay out of my way."

Breaking one foot free of Zander's grasp, he landed a kick in Zander's stomach, knocking him backward. Despite his efforts to regain his foothold, he rolled down the stairs and landed in a heap at the bottom.

Derek desperately tried to open the door, but it was locked. His only escape was to get past Zander and jump to a different time. He turned and looked down the stairwell where Zander was rising to his feet. He bolted down the stairs and rammed Zander into the wall, as he made a mad dash for the time module.

Zander grabbed him before he got to the cabinet and wrestled him to the floor. Derek kicked and clawed at Zander, desperate to free himself and get to the time module. He wiggled out of Zander's grasp and scrambled to his feet. Zander jumped up and grabbed a wine bottle from a rack to his left. He threw it at Derek, hitting him square in the back of the head and knocking him off his feet. The bottle bounced off his head and crashed to the floor, breaking, and spreading wine across the floor.

Derek jumped up and grabbed the back of his head. He was bleeding profusely from the blow. He rushed at Zander and tackled him to the floor.

"I'm going to kill you," he shrieked as he grabbed Zander's neck. Zander deflected his attempt and shoved him backward. Derek fell to the floor and hit his head again. Zander dove at him and grabbed his arm, trying to secure it behind Derek's back. Derek swung at Zander with his other hand, striking him squarely in the jaw. The blow caused Zander to recoil and roll away.

Derek sprinted to the cabinet. He quickly grabbed the handles and disappeared in a flash. Zander rose to his feet and gazed at the mess of blood and wine on the floor. The sound of a key being turned in the basement door startled him, and he realized someone was coming down the stairs. With nowhere to hide, he grabbed the handlebars of the time module and vanished into the future.

Roger, Connor, and young Zander were in the basement when he suddenly appeared in front of them.

"That is so amazing," Connor exclaimed when Zander materialized.

"When is it, right now?" Zander asked, panting from the exertion of fighting with Derek.

"About ten minutes after you left," Roger said.

"I've got to go back and clean up the basement."

"Wait, what happened?" Roger asked.

"When I went back after dropping the body off, I found Derek there. I tried to get him and bring him back, but he got away. I did manage to bloody him up, though," Zander said with a smug smile. "Now I've got to go back and clean up the mess."

"Why didn't you clean it up before you came back?" Connor asked.

"Somebody was coming down, so I had to jump. I'm going to try to jump back a little later and get it cleaned up."

"What if they're still down there when you get back?" Roger asked.

"I guess I'll just jump back."

"That will be quite a show for them," Roger laughed.

"It's a risk I'll have to take."

Zander adjusted the knob on the time module and grabbed the handles. He managed to land back in 1920 alone. He quickly cleaned up the mess and jumped back to his own time.

Chapter Ten

Backward and Forward in Time

Jake was still struggling with his trust dilemma when he awoke in the morning. He was pretty sure that Zander was telling the truth, but he couldn't be certain. His mind kept trying to work out the problem, but he kept coming to the same solution. He was going to have to go forward in time to see who really invented the time module. He really hoped it was Zander. His single encounter with Derek made his skin crawl. There seemed to be something sinister, even maniacal about him.

Unfortunately, Jake didn't know how to use the machine. Somehow, he needed to get Zander to show it to him and teach him how it worked. He thought through the problem as he showered, shaved, and got dressed. He was lost in thought while he ate breakfast.

"What's on your mind?" Mia asked, noticing how quiet he was.

"Oh," Jake said, awkwardly. "Just thinking about the stuff I have to do today."

"And what's that?"

"Just the usual, you know, checking on my guys and making sure they're on task."

Jake put his dishes in the sink and kissed his wife as he walked to the door. "Bye, honey," he said as he opened the door. "Love you."

"Love you too," she called out as the door closed.

Jake drove around the corner and parked in front of the old house. He strolled up to the door with tools in hand, rang the doorbell and stepped back. Soon, Zander opened the door.

"Jake," he said in a surprised tone. "What's up?"

"Uh, well," Jake stammered nervously. "Before you moved in, I was supposed to fix up some things in the house. I have some time this morning so I was wondering if I could work on some stuff for a few hours."

"Absolutely," Zander responded, waiving his arm in a sweeping gesture. "Please come in."

"Thanks," Jake said as he stepped inside.

"What are you going to work on?" Zander asked with a broad smile on his face. It was as if he already knew why Jake was really there and was just playing along.

"The, uh, plumbing in the downstairs bathroom," Jake stammered. He hadn't planned out his story very well and was making it up as he went. "Yeah, the downstairs bathroom has some plumbing problems," Jake said, nervously. He wasn't sure if he was nervous about being caught trying to use the time module, or if he was worried that Zander might really be the killer and might do something drastic if he thought Jake knew the truth.

"Well, I'll be working in the office right over here," Zander said. "Let me know if you need anything."

Jake nodded as Zander turned and walked back to the office. He headed for the bathroom to pretend like he was fixing something. He turned on the sink and flushed the toilet. They were working fine. He turned on the shower. Water flowed freely from the shower head and swirled down the drain. There were no plumbing problems in the bathroom.

He walked down the hall to the office where he expected to see Zander, but he wasn't there. He walked to the basement door. It was open. He called out to Zander to see if he was down there.

"Yeah, Jake," I'm down here," Zander replied.

Jake walked down the steps to the basement. About halfway down he pulled a pipe wrench out of his toolbelt just in case Zander was waiting to jump him at the bottom of the stairs. His heart started beating faster and harder as an anxious knot in his stomach began to grow. He was beginning to think it had been a mistake to come over to the old house alone. He reached the bottom of the stairs and peered around the corner, pipe wrench in hand. Zander was standing by the time module looking at him.

"It's okay, Jake," Zander said, reassuringly, "I think I know why you're really here. Why don't you put the pipe wrench down and come over here? I'll show you how this thing works."

Jake was surprised at Zander's candor. He acted like he had nothing to hide. But that might be an act to lure Jake in. At this point, he didn't feel like he had any other choice but to cooperate and hope for the best. He set the wrench down and walked slowly toward Zander.

When Jake was about five feet away, Zander held up his hand, motioning for Jake to stop.

"See that line on the floor?" he asked, pointing to the floor just in front of Jake.

Jake looked at the floor and noticed a line that appeared to have been drawn with chalk. As he followed the line with his eyes, he realized that it formed a box around the time module.

"You have to be standing inside this box in order for the time module to pull you through time," Zander continued. "Honestly, I don't know why it works that way, but it does. We've figured this out through trial and error. We've also learned through experience that straddling the line is very dangerous."

Zander certainly spoke with authority. Jake wanted to trust him, but he felt that he had to be sure. He wondered if Zander already knew his intention. Had he already made a time jump and didn't remember it?

"Come a little closer," Zander said, shaking Jake from his thoughts. "Let me show you the time module. I know you've already seen it but let me show you how it works," Zander said as he turned slightly and motioned toward the cabinet. Then he paused and turned back to Jake. "You have to promise that you will not try to use this without my supervision, Jake. Do you agree to that?"

Jake nodded, realizing that his mouth was gaping open in amazement. "Yeah, of course," he replied without thinking of the consequences.

"Okay, now step over here so you can see the controls," Zander said as Jake huddled in closer. "This dial is the time meter. You see I have handwritten approximate dates on it," Zander said, running his finger around the dial to show the markings, "I've figured out time positions of the dial by making time jumps. They're really just approximations but you can get pretty close to the time you're targeting by setting it and making small adjustments." Zander stopped talking and looked at Jake. A broad smile crossed his face. "Do you want to make a jump?" he asked.

Jake stared at the controls and back at Zander. "You mean, right now?" he asked.

"Yes," Zander replied. "Right now. Why not?"

"Okay," Jake said. "Where are we going to go?"

"You mean, where in time?" Zander said with a smile. "Let's go back in time a little. I want to show you something. Huddle up close, now, it's very important to stay well within the line I drew on the floor."

Jake stepped closer to the time module, looking at his feet to make sure he was well inside the box. Zander turned the knob slightly counterclockwise, then put his left hand on the left handlebar.

"When I put my right hand on the other bar," he said. "I will complete the circuit and the module, and this house will transport us back in time. Ready?" Zander asked.

Jake just nodded his head. Zander grabbed the other bar and Jake felt a sudden feeling sweep through him like the feeling in the pit of your stomach when going down a slide or falling. He heard a vague motor sound somewhere in the distance. Just as suddenly as it started, the feeling of motion and the distant motor sound stopped.

"Okay," Zander said proudly. "Here we are."

"Where are we?" Jake asked. "Or I guess I should say, 'when are we,' right?"

"Exactly," Zander said enthusiastically. "I've taken us back to the day your sister-in-law died."

"What?" Jake demanded. "Why?"

"Because I want you to see what happened. We've got to be careful not to be seen. If I timed it right, it's about five o'clock in the evening. We're going to go upstairs and hide where we can see what happens, but not be seen by you or your family."

Zander led the way to the top of the stairs. It was dark. Jake remembered that the lights were out in the basement that night. The basement had a distinct musty smell that Jake recognized from the time he and Thomas went down there together. Most likely, the smell was the result of being closed off the whole time Thomas and his family lived there.

Jake and Zander were about halfway up the stairs when Jake suddenly had a thought.

"Zander," he whispered. "Wait a minute."

Jake pulled out his cell phone and activated the flashlight. He shined it up the stairs in front of them. There was a heavy layer of dust on the stairs but no footprints. He turned and shined his light down the stairs behind him. Two sets of footprints were imprinted in the dusty steps.

"Oh my gosh," Jake quietly gasped.

"You're just now figuring out that it was you and me that made the footprints on the stairs you and Thomas will find later tonight?" Zander asked with a smirk.

"Uh, yup!" Jake replied, trying to sound sarcastically stupid.

They tiptoed to the top of the stairs. Zander pulled a skeleton key out of his pocket and quietly inserted it into the lock. He opened the door slightly and peered out. Jake could hear Mia and Janet talking in the kitchen. He could hear Thomas talking and the kids playing in the backyard.

"We're going to go around to the front room and out the front door," Zander whispered. "Stay with me."

The two men crouched as they quietly tiptoed toward the front of the house. Once they were outside, Zander sprinted down the front walkway and out onto the sidewalk. Jake's heart skipped a few beats as he broke into a dead run to catch up to his sneaky companion. They made their way around to the corner and ducked into an ally that slithered behind the houses on the block. When they arrived at the back fence of the old house, Zander crawled through a small broken section and hid in the bushes.

"You really know your way around this place," Jake whispered as he crawled up next to Zander.

"We're going to be here a while," Zander said quietly, ignoring Jake's comment. "So just get comfortable and watch.

Jake watched the events of that fateful night unfold in front of him as he and Zander hid in the bushes. He listened to his conversation with Thomas about the house being haunted and hearing voices in the house at night. Finally, he and Thomas went to check on the basement. While they were gone, Mia and Janet started to clear the table. The kids went in the house and turned on the TV.

While the women were inside, someone cautiously approached the backyard from the other side and poured something into Janet's glass. Then he quickly disappeared into the shadows. Janet came out to clear more dishes. She picked up her glass and gulped down the rest of the lemonade she had been drinking. Within moments she was on the ground, writhing uncontrollably. Jake watched her final moments as Mia came out, found her on the ground and screamed for help.

"That's our cue," Zander said as he turned and crawled back into the ally. He seemed completely unaffected by the murder they had just witnessed. Jake followed him with tears streaming down his cheeks. He had just witnessed the murder of his sister-in-law, and now he had seen the man who did it: Derek Killian. Zander had wanted him to see it so he would know who the killer was and that he could trust Zander.

Jake silently followed Zander's lead back down to the basement. With everybody outside attending to Janet, it was easy to sneak back in through the front door and down to the basement. Zander turned the knob back to the right and looked back at Jake, who was making sure he was completely inside the hand-drawn box on the floor.

"Ready?" Zander asked.

"Yeah," Jake said, dryly.

Zander grabbed the handlebars and Jake felt the lifting motion in his stomach as the pair made the jump back to the time they left.

"What do you think of that?" Zander chuckled. "Your first trip through time."

Jake was still panting from the adrenaline. "

"We just witnessed a murder, and you act like we had a pleasant day at the park."

Zander sighed. "I'm sorry," he replied, realizing that he should have been more considerate of Jake's feelings. "You're right! I got caught up in the excitement and forgot that this hits very close to home for you. I got so excited to prove that Derek was the bad guy that I lost sight of the trauma that night caused for you and your family. I am truly sorry, Jake!"

Jake's nerves began to calm. Zander had just proven his innocence and that Derek was the killer.

"Apology accepted," Jake said, "Now how do we get this bastard?"

"Like I said before, he's going to try and kill Bridget at the wedding. We need to catch him there, hopefully just before the wedding starts so that we don't make a scene and the wedding isn't ruined by violence."

"I'm feeling pretty good about violence right about now," Jake said, feeling hostility toward Derek growing inside him.

"Look," Zander said, putting a hand on Jake's shoulder. "I know it's hard, but we've got to keep our senses about us. Derek is a cunning and dangerous man. Don't underestimate him. He's outsmarted me repeatedly as I've chased him through time. We've got to work together on this."

"Okay," Jake said reluctantly. "What's the next step?"

"Why don't you go home and spend some time with your wife or go see Thomas. Do something to take your mind off it. I know it must be hard living that day all over again."

Jake nodded. "Yeah, that sounds like a good idea." He picked up his toolbelt and trudged up the stairs. He was still blinking tears from his eyes after watching the tragic events that led to the death of his sister-in-law. He climbed in his truck and looked at his watch. It was four o'clock in the afternoon. They time-jumped in the morning but now it was late afternoon. Why didn't they come back to the same time they left? What happened during those hours that were now lost from Jake's life? Did he somehow live them on a different timeline? A multitude of questions were swirling around his mind and only one man could answer them.

He turned off the ignition in his truck and walked back up the walkway to the front door. He rang the doorbell. No answer. He rang it again two more times with no answer. Finally, he opened the door and peered inside. "Zander?" he called out, expecting to hear Zander reply. No reply came. He called out again. Still, no reply.

Fearing something had happened to Zander, he entered the house, calling out Zander's name. He checked every room, but Zander wasn't there. Finally, he walked down the stairs to the basement. Again, Zander was not there. The only thing in the basement was the time module and the cabinet that housed it. Jake stood silently staring at the machine as he considered his options. His original plan was to secretly jump forward in time to see who really invented time travel. Now, he considered jumping forward to stop Derek before he jumped back in time and killed Janet.

He walked across the floor to the cabinet and opened the door. He looked intently at the time module, wondering if he really could make it work. Curiosity was getting the better of him. He rubbed his finger along the dial, examining the markings that Zander had made on it, indicating time periods both in the future and the past. His finger stopped on a marking in the future.

"This is the furthest one forward," he muttered to himself. "This must be the point in time Zander started from."

He put his hand on the dial and cautiously moved it forward to the last mark. He removed his hand from the dial and looked at it for a moment. 'Maybe,' he thought to himself, rubbing his chin. 'Just maybe I could move it back a little bit and get there before Derek kills anybody.'

He reached for the dial and moved it carefully to the left a few notches. He put his left hand on the left handlebar. He took a deep breath and placed his right hand on the other bar. Instantly, he felt the rush coursing through his body as he hurtled forward in time. It felt as if every nerve in his body was ignited with electricity. He heard engines humming in the distant background. He felt the sensation of falling. Then suddenly, the motion he felt coursing through his body stopped. He had arrived at his destination in the future.

He removed his hands from the time module and turned around. To his surprise, Derek Killian was standing behind him, holding a baseball bat.

"Hi Jake, "Derek said as a twisted smile formed on his lips. "I've been waiting for you."

Without another word, Derek thrust the bat forward, catching Jake in the abdomen. The force of the blow drove him backward, crashing into the time module. Jake quickly regained his balance and assumed a fighting stance.

"Now you find out the truth; our time dance did start with a murder… yours," Derek said, pointing a finger at Jake. "But what's going to drive you crazy is whether it was the first thing that happened or if it happens somewhere in the middle. The fact that I knew you were coming and already know your name has got to make you wonder. But you're not going to have much time to wonder," Derek said as he raised the bat. He laughed a hideous laugh, the laugh of a madmen intent upon murder.

Jake was dumbfounded, "You can't kill me," he panted, "I'm your ancestor. If I die, then you don't exist."

"Wrong," Derek shrieked. He lowered the bat slightly and composed himself. "That would be true if I killed you before you had offspring, but guess what?" he asked, his pitch rising with hysterical excitement. He paused as if he really expected Jake to answer.

Finally, Jake asked, "What?"

"Guess," Derek squealed.

"I don't know what you're talking about," Jake responded.

"Mia's going to have a baby," Derek said with maniacal delight.

"Well, that's news to me," Jake said. "She hasn't said anything about it, so I don't think you know – "

"Oh, I know," Derek insisted, raising the bat over his head, "I am a pretty good detective, after all."

Jake realized that his only chance to survive was to rush Derek and close the gap before the bat hit him. Just as he lunged forward and Derek raised the bat to make the fatal blow, the deafening sound of a gunshot rang out. Derek dropped the bat as he staggered forward and collided with Jake. Both men fell to the floor. Derek quickly rolled toward the time module. Without wasting a second, he pulled himself up, adjusted the dial and grabbed the handles. He was gone in an instant.

Jake looked up from his prone position on the basement floor and saw Zander standing across the room holding a shotgun, smoke still escaping from the barrel. Jake sat up and looked at him.

"So, the man who was murdered was me," Jake said, trying to catch his breath.

"Yes," Zander said gravely.

"Why didn't you tell me?" Jake asked, shaking his head.

"I did tell you not to use the time module without me," Zander said.

"When did you know I was the victim?" Jake asked.

"Well, obviously, I didn't know right away. Nobody could identify you at first because you weren't from this time."

"Derek already knew me when I arrived," Jake said. "So, I'm guessing this isn't the first time this happened."

Zander sighed. "It turns out that when you start jumping through time, there really isn't a first and second time anymore. It all just seems to get jumbled together."

"Whatever," Jake said. "I'm not even going to try to wrap my head around that."

"But, no, this was not the first time this has happened," Zander said. "That's why I was able to prevent it. And I suppose that's also why Derek was wearing a bulletproof vest."

Zander offered Jake his hand to help him off the floor.

"Come on, Jake," he said. "Let's get you back to your time. We have a killer to catch. And we're going to catch him at your brother's wedding."

Chapter Eleven

Bridezilla

"I don't know, Jake," Thomas mumbled pensively as he stared at the wall. "It feels like I'm being unfaithful to Janet."

"Life goes on, Thomas," Jake said, trying to be helpful. But he didn't really know how to help his older brother.

They were sitting in the living room of Jake's house discussing Thomas' upcoming wedding. Jake wasn't sure if Thomas was really feeling disloyal to his deceased wife or if he just had cold feet, but he was certain that Thomas was concerned about Bridget's expensive taste.

"Am I doing the right thing?" Thomas questioned.

"Well, how do the kids feel about her?" Jake asked.

"They like her okay," Thomas replied. "And I think she's really good with them."

"Are there other issues that are causing you to question your decision to marry Bridget?"

"Maybe," Thomas answered. "She wants a really expensive wedding and I'm afraid I can't afford it. Her wedding dress is expensive, the venue is expensive, the catering is expensive…"

"Have you talked to her about your concerns?"

"No," Thomas whined. "I don't want her to be disappointed with the wedding."

"Yeah, but if you can't afford it, that's going to put a strain on your marriage before you even get married. What about her parents, can't they help with the cost?"

"Maybe," Thomas said. "But we haven't talked to them about it. I told her that I would just cover the cost, but I didn't expect it to be this expensive. She acts like money is no object. It started with the wedding ring. She thought that I should spend three months' salary on it. I just think that's way too much money, especially when I'm paying for the wedding."

The brothers' conversation was interrupted by Mia and Bridget returning from shopping. Bridget was young and bubbly. Jake and Mia thought she talked too much. Sometimes they felt as if she talked at them instead of with them. As usual, when they came through the door, Bridget was talking quickly, and Mia was silent.

"I used to wear those when I was in high school," Bridget rattled at top speed. "But I just can't wear them anymore, know what I mean?" She didn't wait for Mia to answer. "I look back at high school pictures and I just can't believe the clothes I used to wear. I think my taste has matured or something because the old stuff I used to wear is just so..." she waived her hands in the air while she searched for the right word. Finally, she found it. "Yesterday!"

"Hi ladies," Jake said as Bridget took a breath.

"Whatcha been doin'?" Thomas asked.

"Hi, honey," Bridget said as she rushed across the floor to hug her fiancé. She didn't seem to notice his dismal mood.

"We've been looking at bridesmaid dresses," Mia managed to say before Bridget took over.

"Oh, we found the perfect dresses," Bridget said gleefully. "And they're even the right color because you know I wanted all my bridesmaids to wear cinnamon rose-colored dresses, except for the maid of honor, her dress needs to be a little more special than the bridesmaids, so I want the color to be just a little deeper than the cinnamon-rose, but I don't know what that color is called. I guess we'll have to ask someone at the store."

She pulled out her cellphone as she approached Thomas who was slouched on the couch with his feet up on the coffee table. She scrolled her finger up and down on her cellphone screen, looking for pictures she took of the dresses as she nestled up next to him.

"See," she said nudging Thomas. "This is the dress we found. See the color? That's the color I want. And see how the shape is asymmetrical with a v-neck lined with these ruffles? That's exactly what I want."

"Looks great, honey," Thomas said as though he were in pain. Although Bridget didn't notice it, he wasn't looking at the dress she was showing him. All he could see was the cost.

"Oh," Bridget exclaimed, bubbling over with enthusiasm. "I found the perfect wedding dress and I want you to come look at it. Or is it bad luck for you to see the dress before the wedding? Does anybody know?"

Jake shrugged, Thomas ignored the question and Bridget continued before Mia had a chance to say anything.

"So maybe you shouldn't come look at the dress, but Mia has seen it, what did you think Mia?"

"I think it's great, just as long as you're happy with it."

"How much is it?" Thomas asked, gulping.

"Honey," Bridget said in a mildly scolding tone. "That's not a question you should ask."

"It is if I have to pay for it," Thomas said, dryly.

"Oh, I forgot to tell you," Bridget said. "My mom said she would pay for it."

"Does she know how much it costs?" Thomas asked.

"Yes," Bridget said. "She knows this is a once in a lifetime event, so she wants everything to be perfect."

Thomas was mildly relieved but also annoyed. He and Bridget were opposites when it came to money. Thomas was frugal, Bridget was extravagant. He and Janet had been more like-minded about money. The closer they got to the wedding the more he found himself missing his deceased wife.

"Oh, I forgot to tell you," Bridget said with her usual enthusiasm. "We have appointments with the venue, the caterer and the bakery on Saturday. It's going to be a full day of wedding planning. I'm so excited!"

"Can't wait," Thomas muttered under his breath.

Saturday arrived and Thomas drove to Bridget's home to pick her up for their day of wedding planning. Bridget had recently finished college and had moved back into her parent's home. She had not found a job following graduation. In fact, she hadn't even tried.

Thomas had begun to wonder if he was so caught up in their whirlwind romance that he had not considered some red flags about her character. Her parents were wealthy and lived in a large house in a gated community. Bridget was an only child and had grown up with everything she wanted. Thomas made good money, but he worried that it wouldn't be enough to keep Bridget in the lifestyle she was accustomed to.

He walked slowly up to the front door and rang the doorbell. Instead of Bridget answering the door as he had hoped, her mother, Fran, came to the door. Bridget's parents were in their thirties when they had their one and only child. Fran was now in her mid-fifties and was gracefully going grey. The front edges of her hair were yellowed from years of heavy smoking.

"Thomas," she said in a raspy tone that betrayed her smoking habit. "Please come in. Bridget is getting ready. She'll be down in a minute. I'm so excited about today."

Thomas felt awkward around Fran. Although she didn't come right out and say it, she made comments that made him feel like she didn't think he made enough money. But her next comment made him wonder if his marriage to Bridget was going to be a total mistake.

"Thomas," Fran said. "With you and Bridget starting a new life together, I wonder if it might be a good idea to have the wedding be just about you and her."

"Well, it is just about her and me," Thomas replied. "What else would it be about?"

"Well, you have two children and while I know they're part of the package that comes with you, I just wonder if maybe the children should be left out of the wedding, you know so that you and Bridget can focus on each other for that special day."

Thomas was dumbfounded. "You're seriously suggesting that I should not include my children in the wedding?"

"Well, children can be disruptive, and I don't want anything to spoil this special occasion."

Fortunately, Thomas didn't have time to answer before Bridget came bounding down the stairs. She rushed up to him, smothering him in a tight hug and showering him with kisses.

"My mom is coming with us today," she said excitedly. "I hope that's okay."

"Of course," Thomas replied, choking on his words. What else could he say? He knew better than to object.

"Why don't we take my car?" Fran suggested. "I'll drive so you two can discuss wedding details."

On the way to their first appointment with the venue, Bridget and her mother discussed the wedding while Thomas sat quietly looking out the window. Occasionally, Bridget would ask him a question, but would not wait for him to answer before she asked her mother for her opinion. Thomas was wondering why they even wanted him along. He was beginning to feel like he was nothing more than an invited guest to the wedding, even though he was the groom.

The meeting at the venue was no different. Fran pulled up in front and handed her keys to the valet while Bridget and Thomas made their way to the entrance. They were met at the door by their wedding consultant who was almost as bubbly and enthusiastic as Bridget. Fran hurried to catch up and met the group in the lobby. After a tour of the facility, they retreated to the consultant's office to work out details. Naturally, Bridget wanted the most extravagant package. Thomas felt his stomach tighten as he watched the price tag skyrocket. He finally broke his silence.

"Time out," he called out as he jammed the fingers of his right hand into the palm of his left hand. "I'm sorry to be a party pooper but this is just way more than I can afford. Can't we find a lower-priced package?"

There was dead silence for a moment as the bride, her mother and the consultant stared at Thomas. Finally, Fran cleared her throat and spoke.

"Thomas, we're not expecting you to pay for all this. I'm planning to pay for it."

"Oh," Thomas said sheepishly. "I didn't know there was a change of plan." He felt foolish for his outburst, but he still felt as though he was being left out of the planning. And he was simmering about Fran's suggestion to exclude his kids from the wedding.

"I told you mother was going to pay for it," Bridget said taking his hand. "Don't you remember?

"No," Thomas replied. "When did you tell me?"

"When we were talking about the wedding dress."

"I thought you were only talking about the dress," Thomas said defensively. "I didn't know you meant the whole wedding."

"You know I've always dreamed of the perfect wedding and when mother and I realized you couldn't afford what I wanted, she offered to pay for everything." Her tone suddenly changed from somber and reassuring to exuberant. "And it's going to be perfect don't you think? I'm so excited."

She didn't wait for Thomas to answer. She immediately turned back to the consultant and locked in her choices for the wedding. Once the venue and catering order was confirmed they made their way to the cake studio to sample cakes.

The cake consultant seated them at a table and brought out samples for them to try. Bridget and her mother sampled them and chattered about the various flavors and which ones they liked the best. Thomas sat quietly wondering why he was there since Bridget and her mother were clearly not interested in his opinions or input. Finally, he got up and walked out of the cake studio. They had spent half the day at the venue and hadn't taken time to eat, and he was hungry. He walked into a deli next to the cake studio and ordered a sandwich.

Thirty minutes later Bridget turned to ask Thomas a question. She was shocked to find he wasn't sitting next to her.

"Where did Thomas go?" she asked as she looked around the cake shop.

"He got up and left a while ago," the cake consultant said. "I thought you knew."

"What a rude thing to do," Fran said. "It's his wedding too. You would think he would want to be involved in the planning."

Bridget pulled out her phone and called his number. Thomas answered.

"Honey, where did you go?" she asked.

"I clearly wasn't needed," Thomas replied. "And I was hungry, so I went next door to get a sandwich."

"But I need your opinion," Bridget whined.

"No, you really don't," Thomas replied bitterly. "You and your mother can make all the arrangements and maybe I'll just show up for the wedding, okay?"

"That's not how I want it to be," Bridget whimpered. "This is our wedding, and we should both be involved in the decisions."

"But we're not," Thomas replied, "You and your mom are making them and that's fine. She is paying for it after all."

"Don't be that way," Bridget shot back. "Come over here and sample the cake mother and I picked out. You're going to love it."

"That's what I mean," Thomas said. "You guys already made the decision, and you just want me to be okay with it. What if I hate the cake you picked out?"

"Oh, you won't hate it," Bridget promised. "You're going to love it, I'm sure of it."

"I'm sure I will," Thomas submissively replied. "Go ahead and order it.

"Oh, now we're fighting, aren't we?" Bridget whined.

"No," Thomas said with mocking reassurance. "This isn't fighting. This is me concurring with your decisions."

"But you're upset," Bridget said. "I don't want you to be upset."

"The wedding arrangements are much more important to you than they are to me, so whatever you want is fine with me."

"Really?" Bridget asked, with her usual perkiness returning.

"Really!" Thomas said. "I'm just a third wheel today. I think you would have a much better day checking this stuff out with your mother."

"Are you sure?" Bridget asked.

"Yeah, I'm sure. I'm going to call Jake to pick me up, okay?"

"Okay," Bridget said. "If you're sure."

"I'm sure," Thomas said.

"Okay, sweetie. I love you!" Bridget said.

"I love you too," Thomas said as he ended the call.

Jake came right over to pick him up. He could tell there was something wrong by the tone in Thomas' voice when he called. Thomas was waiting on the curb when he rolled up in front of the sandwich shop.

"What's going on?" Jake asked as Thomas jumped into the car.

"Drive, bro!" Thomas ordered as he slammed the door. "I need to get away from this place fast."

"What happened?" Jake asked as they drove away.

"I think I'm making a huge mistake, Jake," Thomas moaned.

"Why, what happened?"

"Well, the day started with Bridget's mom telling me she thought I should not have my kids at the wedding."

"Are you kidding me?" Jake asked. "Why?

"She thinks that the marriage and celebration should just be between me and Bridget, and the kids can get involved afterward."

"That's the stupidest thing I've ever heard," Jake retorted. "What's wrong with that lady?

"Everything," Thomas said. "I actually can't find a single thing I like about her. She's domineering; she's opinionated and arrogant; she looks down on me because I'm not made of money like she is…

But I make good money, Jake. It's not like I'm poor. I make good money!"

"I know you do," Jake replied sympathetically.

"I just don't know if I'm rich enough to support Bridget in the lifestyle she's used to. Every time I turn around, the money issue comes up: I don't make enough to afford the wedding she wants; my house isn't as grand as the one she grew up in; I drive a Volvo instead of a Mercedes. The list goes on and on."

Jake was at a loss for words. Under normal circumstances he would tell Thomas to break things off with Bridget and cancel the wedding, but he knew there was a future for them. At this point, however, he didn't see how they were going to make it to the wedding day.

*****

Zander rubbed his forehead as he listened to Jake rehearse Thomas' experience with his fiancé and future mother-in-law.

"So, the mother doesn't want Thomas' kids at the wedding, wow!" Zander said as Jake finished the story.

"Yeah," Jake responded. "That's kind of a deal breaker, wouldn't you say?"

"Under normal circumstances, yes, I would say that's definitely a deal breaker. But I think there are some time fragments at play here."

"What kind of time fragments would cause this?" Jake asked.

"You know this isn't their first time through the wedding. I don't want to get into details, but it might not have worked out so well for the kids last time. We've got to change that this time around."

"So, the kids got hurt last time, is that what you're saying?"

"If they had, then that would certainly cause Bridget's mother to want to keep them away, even if she doesn't know the real reason for her feelings."

"From what I've heard, she doesn't have any feelings."

"That's not true," Zander said. "She's really a good woman and things wouldn't be the way they are now, if I wasn't chasing a madman through time who is intent on killing Thomas and his fiancé."

"Time fragments," Jake said. "You're saying that time fragments have caused all the drama for the wedding party?"

"Yes," Zander said. "It wasn't like this before."

"How is it going to be different now?" Jake demanded. "If it's all happened before, it sounds to me like it always ends the same."

"What's different this time," Zander said calmy. "Is you!"

"Me?" Jake asked, taken aback. "How so?"

"I'm hoping that your involvement will change the outcome. You were not involved before."

"I wasn't at the wedding?"

"You were at the wedding, but you were not involved in the effort to stop Killian. You and I had not met. I'm trying something new this time around and I think it will work. At least I hope it will."

"So, what am I supposed to do?" Jake asked.

"First, you need to make sure your brother goes through with the wedding. If we can change the outcome and restore it to what it was meant to be, then everything should be fine. Thomas and Bridget will have a good marriage that generations later will eventually lead to me. In other words, Jake, if we don't salvage this marriage, I will cease to exist."

*****

Thomas and Bridget were sitting on opposite ends of the couch in Jake and Mia's living room. Bridget sat with her arms folded. Her right leg was draped over her left leg and was bouncing up and down. Thomas was slouched over on the other side of the couch as if he had been emotionally beaten down. Jake and Mia were sitting on the other couch, facing the unhappy couple.

After the wedding planning fiasco, Thomas had become emotionally distant from Bridget. He wouldn't share his concerns with her because he felt that he wouldn't be heard and that nothing would change. Bridget was so wrapped up in planning her perfect wedding that she was completely blind to how it was affecting her fiancé. Jake had convinced Mia that they had to try to bring Thomas and Bridget back together.

"Thank you both for coming over tonight," he said. "I know things have gotten a little crazy, and I think maybe if you guys can talk about it – "

"She doesn't want my kids at the wedding," Thomas blurted out, interrupting Jake.

Bridget uncrossed her legs and leaned forward, "What?" She said in a demanding tone. "I never said I didn't want your kids at the wedding. Where did you get that idea?"

"From your mother," Thomas sneered. "When I went to pick you up for all the wedding planning stuff, your mother told me that we shouldn't have the kids at the wedding because the day should be all about us."

Bridget was silent for a moment as she thought about what Thomas said.

"Oh my gosh," she said, breaking her silence. "I think I know how this happened. I told my mother that I was worried about the kids being at the wedding because you and I would be distracted by the ceremony and the guests and all the usual wedding stuff and wouldn't be able to keep an eye on them. I just meant that we needed to make sure someone was watching them. I guess my mother thought I meant that I didn't want them at the wedding at all."

Thomas began to warm up a little. "So, you don't mind if they're at the wedding?"

"Of course not," Bridget giggled. "They're our kids. They have to be there."

Bridget referring to them as 'our kids,' instead of, 'your kids,' felt reassuring to Thomas.

"That makes me feel better," he said. "I'm still afraid of your mother, though."

"I'll talk to her and clear this up," Bridget laughed, "she's really not the dragon lady you make her out to be."

"Are you sure?" Thomas whispered.

"Yes, I'm sure," Bridget replied. After a brief pause, she asked, "Are we good now? Can I scoot over close to you?"

"Not yet," was the disappointing reply. "There's something else."

Bridget braced herself for what was coming next. "Okay," she said, quietly.

"I just don't feel like I've had any part in planning our wedding and seeing how expensive it's going to be makes me feel like I'm not going to be able to support you in the lifestyle your used to. I'm just afraid I'm going to disappoint you."

Bridget's head dropped as she realized how her actions had affected her fiancé.

"Thomas, I love you and I'm sorry," she said. "I guess I got so caught up in the wedding that I lost focus of what's really important

– you and me and our family. I don't have to have an extravagant wedding; okay, maybe I've been dreaming of that my whole life, but if you want to have a smaller wedding, I'm fine with that. I'm sorry I made you feel this way."

"Really?" Thomas asked, managing a slight smile.

"Yes, really?" she replied, returning his smile.

Jake breathed a sigh of relief as he watched his brother and future sister-in-law patch things up. Bridget scooted up against Thomas and giggled when he put his arm around her. Jake began to realize that Bridget wasn't the person he thought she was. Maybe things would work out after all.

Chapter Twelve

The Wedding

"Should I really go through with this?" Thomas asked Jake as he tugged at his bow tie. "I just feel so nervous."

"Yes, Thomas," Jake said, pointing his finger at his brother. "You're going through with this. You're lucky to have Bridget."

"Yeah, I know."

Thomas had agreed to the extravagant wedding Bridget and her mother had planned after she calmed his fears about money. He was grateful that he didn't have to foot the bill and decided to just enjoy it.

Thomas and Jake were in the Groom's room getting ready for the ceremony. Mia was watching Thomas' children and was waiting with them outside the wedding chapel. The kids were to be the ring bearers for the ceremony and were excited to play their role in the wedding.

A knock at the door interrupted the brothers' conversation. Jake opened the door to find Zander standing there.

"The perimeter is secure," Zander said. "I think we're ready for the ceremony."

"The perimeter is secure?" Thomas repeated, mockingly. "Is this a wedding or a military operation."

"It's a wedding, of course," Zander replied. "Our security detail makes sure that only your invited guests are permitted. We also watch over your gift table and make sure your guests don't get out of control after drinking too much."

"Oh," Thomas replied. "I had no idea."

Zander was posing as head of security so that he had a reason to be at the wedding. It was a role Jake suspected Zander had played several times already. Zander had been vague about his plan to prevent murder and mayhem at the wedding. He had just told Jake to stay close to Thomas and keep his eyes open.

"You look familiar," Thomas said, looking at Zander. "Have we met?"

"This is Zander Knox," Jake offered. "He's head of security here."

"And I'm renting your house," Zander said with a smile.

"Oh, yeah," Thomas said. "How is that old dump?"

"It suits me just fine," Zander replied. "I don't mean to rush you, but I think they're ready to begin. Gentlemen, after you," Zander said, motioning toward the wedding chapel down the hall.

Thomas walked out first followed by Jake. As Jake passed by, Zander pulled him aside and shoved something into his hand.

"Take this," he said. "You might need it later."

Jake looked at a strange looking gun in his hand. "What is this?" he asked.

"It's a ray gun," Zander explained. "It will vaporize its target upon impact. I've got one too."

"I thought you said you didn't have ray guns in the future," Jake whispered.

"We don't in my future," Zander replied. "I had to go into the future from my time to get these."

"I don't even know how to use this thing," Jake hissed. "Why didn't you give it to me sooner so I could get used to it?"

"Because I didn't have them sooner," Zander barked. "I just got back with these. It's easy to use. Just point and pull the trigger. The gun will do the rest. Just make sure you know your target."

"When is this supposed to go down?" Jake asked.

"I don't know," Zander answered. "It's different every time.

Jake was unaware that Thomas had walked up behind him until he heard his voice.

"What are you guys talking about?"

Jake jumped a little. "Sorry, Thomas. Zander was just going over some standard security stuff. As the best man, I'm supposed to make sure this goes off without a hitch, I guess."

"Okay," Zander said. "I hear the prelude music playing. Maybe we should get over there."

The brothers walked down the hall to the chapel. Thomas' two kids were waiting outside the chapel doors with Mia. They both hugged their father when they saw him. Thomas and Jake walked to the front of the chapel where the officiator greeted them. Soon the procession started with the bridesmaids and groomsmen, followed by Thomas' children. Finally, the bride came down the aisle, escorted by her father. The moment Thomas saw her in her wedding dress, he knew he had made the right decision.

Throughout the ceremony, Jake kept scanning the room and looking at Zander. He expected Derek to strike at any moment, but nothing happened. The ceremony was perfect, and the bride and groom sealed their marriage with the traditional kiss. As the bride and groom walked back down the aisle as husband and wife, Zander exited the room before them and disappeared into the hallway. Jake kept scanning the attendees looking for Derek's face. He scanned the rafters and still didn't see him. He began to worry that Derek had disguised himself and was one of the attendees.

He hurried out into the hallway to see where Zander went. He didn't understand why the man from the future didn't have more of a plan. If he had been through this before, he should be aware of what was going to happen, but Zander seemed to insinuate that things hadn't gone the same way in past incarnations of the wedding. It almost seemed like Zander was intentionally keeping him in the dark.

Jake scanned the hallway for Zander but didn't see him anywhere. Mia came out with Jeffrey and Tawny on each hand.

"Hi honey," she said cheerily. "Would you like to walk down to the reception area with us?"

"You bet I would," Jake replied. "Let's go."

Jake tried to act calm, even though anxiety was building inside him. He had lost sight of Zander and he felt vulnerable knowing there was a killer lurking close by. To make matters worse, he was worried about the ray gun he had hidden inside his jacket. He had no idea how powerful it was and worried that he might accidentally bump into something and discharge it.

The wedding couple was at the door of the reception area, greeting people as they funneled into the large room. Jake opted to stay with them and suggested that Mia take the kids in and find their table. He would be sitting next to the groom anyway.

At length, the wedding couple took their place at the head table with their wedding party. Dinner came, followed by toasts to the newlyweds. As best man, Jake was expected to make a toast but given the tense circumstances only he and Zander were aware of, he was not in the mood.

Out of duty, he rose from his chair with his goblet in hand and said, "To Thomas, the best brother a guy could ever have. And to Bridget, the best wife my brother could ever hope for. May their marriage be filled with love and harmony."

Jake sat down and the maid of honor stood. She was Bridget's best friend from high school. Jake hadn't met her before the wedding, and he couldn't remember her name. All he knew about her was that she didn't know when to shut up. Maybe it was because of the stress he was feeling with a killer in the crowd, but she really annoyed him. She kept blathering on as her tears washed mascara away from her eyes and down her cheeks. He had no idea what she was saying, and he didn't care. All he cared about was stopping Derek. Zander was still nowhere to be found, which elevated Jake's stress.

Finally, she finished her overexuberant toast and sat down. Then came the first dance. The couple would be on the dance floor all alone. What a perfect opportunity for an assassin, Jake thought. It hadn't occurred to him before, and Zander's absence was making him feel paranoid. He started to question everything. What if Zander and Derek had really been in this together from the start. It would be easy for the two of them to hit the bride and groom together while dancing alone on the dance floor. But then why did Zander give him a weapon? That one was easy. It probably didn't work.

As the couple got up for their first dance, Jake jumped up from his chair and hurried to the edge of the dancefloor. He scoured the crowd for any sign of the assassin. Nothing! No Derek. No Zander. What was going on? Why had Zander disappeared and why hadn't Derek attacked? Then a thought struck him. Maybe Zander got to Derek first and either killed him or captured him and took him back to their time. The thought made him relax a little. Still, not knowing

Zander's fate or Derek's whereabouts made him extremely apprehensive.

The first dance ended, and other couples made their way to the dance floor. With more people dancing, Jake thought the newlyweds would be safe. The logical time to strike would have been during the first dance but nothing happened. It was unlikely that anything would happen now, Jake thought. But then he realized that the killer could be on the dance floor.

With that thought he raced headlong into the throng of dancers and walked around and between the couples looking for Derek and Zander. At this point he couldn't be too careful, and he certainly couldn't assume that Zander wasn't complicit with Derek. Neither of them was on the dance floor. He wasn't sure what to do until he remembered that Zander told him to stay close to the groom.

'What could it hurt?' he thought. 'If there's going to be an attack,' he reasoned, 'the best place for me to be is close to Thomas and Bridget.'

He made his way around the dance floor where Thomas and Bridget were dancing. He hovered so near to them that Bridget began to question his behavior.

"Loosen up Jake," she said, chiding him. "Relax and enjoy the party."

The bouquet and garter toss were uneventful. All the single ladies got into position and when Bridget threw the bouquet behind her, the contest began. As the bouquet rose into the air, the women jockeyed for position to catch it. Two young girls collided as they jumped into the air to get their hands on it. The bouquet just skimmed the tips of their fingers as they bounced away from each other and landed on the floor. It was still up for grabs, and the grabbing began. Women young and old vied for the bundle of flowers, some kicking at it to keep it out of reach of others who were sprawled on the floor in a desperate attempt to snatch it. Finally, a middle-aged woman became the victor and retreated into the crowd with her prize.

The garter toss was a different story. When Thomas shot it off into the crowd the single men in the room acted as though it was poisonous. Nobody wanted to touch it. Instead of clamoring for it, they all eyed it with suspicion as it lay undisturbed on the floor. Finally, a teenage boy picked it up and stuffed it into the shirt pocket of his older brother.

At last, it was time to cut the cake. Jake had remained vigilant in his duty to stay close to Thomas and keep his eyes open. He kept scanning the crowd for any sign of Derek or Zander. The crowd had shrunk significantly since the reception began and Jake estimated that fewer than 70 guests remained. The newlyweds took their position behind the cake as the wedding photographer took pictures. Bridget's father had been drinking a little too much and was staggering toward the table. He stumbled right in front of the bride when a shot rang out. The man fell to the floor and panic gripped the wedding guests.

Jake sprinted to the front of the table and pulled the futuristic gun from his pocket. He saw Derek boldly strolling across the room with a gun in his hand. Jake couldn't safely fire at him without the risk of hitting a wedding guest. Derek continued walking straight toward him and the wedding couple as he raised his weapon and fired again.

Jake heard a voice yelling 'get down' behind him. It was Zander. Jake felt somebody shove him to the floor. As he went down, he heard the bullet whiz past his head and hit something behind him. He rolled back on the floor to see who the bullet had struck. Zander fell to the floor, covered in blood.

"Get him, Jake," Zander hissed, spitting blood as he spoke, "Use the ray gun."

Suddenly, Jake was filled with anger. He rose to his feet and leveled his gun at Derek. When Derek saw the gun in Jake's hand, his eyes widened with fear, and he turned and ran for the door. Jake was trembling with adrenaline as he pulled the trigger. The little gun kicked more than he expected and pulled upward as a tiny blue laser shot out of the barrel, whizzed over Derek's head, and hit a pillar on the far side of the room. The pillar vanished immediately, and part of the ceiling collapsed.

Jake ran out the door of the reception hall just in time to see Derek bolting out the front door of the wedding venue. He ran to the door without thinking of his own safety. Just as he burst through the door to the parking lot a shot rang out and narrowly missed him. The bullet shattered the entry doors and sent glass flying. People inside and outside the building scurried for safety, some ducking behind planters, others dropping to the ground.

Derek turned and ran further into the parking lot. Jake leveled his weapon at Derek and fired off another shot. He watched the blue laser barely miss his target's head and vaporize a car in the parking lot. Derek disappeared into the sea of cars on the lot.

Jake was determined not to let him get away, even if it cost his life. As far as he knew, Zander and Bridget's father were the only casualties so far and the newlywed couple was safe. He was determined to stop Derek and the seemingly endless attempts he had made on Bridget's life as he traveled through time trying to kill her and end Zander's existence.

Jake crept cautiously between the cars as he hunted Derek. His heart was pounding inside his chest. Although he had served in the military, he had never had to face a real opponent like this. He didn't know where Derek was, and he didn't know if Derek knew where he was.

Suddenly, Derek leapt out from behind a car and tackled Jake. As the two of them hit the pavement, Jake lost his grip on his gun, and it went sliding across the pavement. Both he and Derek scrambled for it, each of them trying to shove the other back and grab the gun. Derek elbowed Jake in the face and scrambled past him. In the commotion, Jake suddenly found himself in possession of another gun. He realized that Derek must have lost it as he wrestled with Jake to gain possession of the more powerful futuristic gun.

Derek lunged toward the ray gun, grabbed it, and turned to fire at Jake. To his surprise, Jake already had a weapon and fired before he could shoot. The bullet ripped through Derek's right arm, causing him to drop the ray gun. He turned and scrambled behind a car to get out of the line of fire. Jake picked up the ray gun, then continued to pursue Derek cautiously.

In the dark parking lot, Jake lost sight of him. He heard a car start and speed away. Through the dim light he could see that Derek was behind the wheel. Jake rushed to his truck and followed the car as it sped out of the parking lot and onto the road. He knew the chase would lead him back to the house on the corner. Derek was wounded and Jake knew that he would try to time jump to escape capture.

Jake managed to close the gap between his truck and Derek's car as the two sped toward the old house. By the time they arrived, Jake was right behind him. Derek practically fell out of the car when the door opened. His arm was covered in blood and the loss of blood seemed to be slowing him down. He quickly got to his feet and sprinted to the front door. Jake ran up the walkway behind him but wasn't able to grab him before he went through the front door and slammed it shut. Jake rammed his body into the door, and it burst open easier than he anticipated, causing him to fall to the floor. He jumped to his feet and chased Derek down the stairs to the basement. He knew he had to stop him before he reached the time module.

Derek ran toward the cabinet and reached for the handlebars. Jake lunged at him and landed on the floor with his arms around Derek's legs, which caused Derek to fall toward the machine in front of him. He grabbed the handlebars in a desperate move to prevent himself from bashing his head against the cabinet.

The moment both of Derek's hands made contact with the handle bars the machine was activated. But Jake was holding Derek's legs down on the other side of the safety line. Derek realized the danger he was in and screamed as the machine lit up, but it was happening too fast for him to let go. When the time jump occurred, Derek's body was severed in half. The upper part was transferred to another time and lower half fell to the floor in front of Jake.

Jake reeled backward in horror as he saw Derek's body severed in two. He sat on the floor panting from the exertion and excitement. As he looked upon Derek's severed torso in front of him, he wondered where the other half went. Then the realization that he'd won the battle settled in.

"That's really disgusting!" Jake was startled to hear a kid's voice behind him. He whirled around to find a young boy standing at the bottom of the stairs. "Who is that?" the boy demanded.

"How did you get in here kid?" Jake asked, annoyed that the boy snuck up on him. "You shouldn't be down here."

"I live here," the boy responded.

"Who are you?" Jake demanded.

"Zander Knox," the boy declared.

"No way," Jake said. "There can't be two of you here."

"Where's the older Zander?" young Zander asked, innocently.

"He's over at the wedding venue," Jake said, trying not to upset the boy by telling him that the older version of himself might be dead.

"Did he get shot again?" young Zander asked.

Jake paused and looked at the boy. He was amazed at how calm the kid was considering the gory corpse that lay in front of him.

"Yeah, kid," Jake said. "He got shot tonight."

"I guess I'm going to have to go get him," the boy sighed, shaking his head.

"Is that Derek?" the boy asked, pointing to the severed torso on the floor.

"Yep," Jake replied curtly. "Half of him, anyway."

The time module began to whir and shake and suddenly there were two men standing in front of it. They looked down and saw the severed corpse on the floor and recoiled from it, gasping from the gory sight. Then they looked around the room and saw young Zander standing at the bottom of the stairs.

"You alright, kid?" one of them asked.

"Yeah, I'm fine," the boy replied. "This guy just killed Derek Killian," he said, pointing to Jake, who was still sitting in the middle of the floor.

"Yeah, we know," the other man said. "The top half of him just showed up at the lab."

"So, does that mean that it's over?" Jake asked. "Is he really dead for good or can he somehow come back again?"

"He's dead for good," the boy answered. "The old man and I made sure of that. Derek was apparently a foster child that lived with my family. I never knew him personally, because it came a little later than my time jump, but the older version of myself traveled back to a time before Derek came to live with us and convinced my parents not to take him in. That altered the future so that he never knew us and never came to the lab and killed…" the boy paused as he looked at Jake. "Holy crap," he exclaimed. "You're the one he killed, aren't you?"

Jake only nodded and beckoned for the boy to continue his story.

So, anyway," the boy continued. "The original Derek had already time jumped so he was still out there. We realized that we couldn't just capture him and bring him back for trial because we had altered his future after his time jump, which means that now the murder he committed in the future never happened. If we took him back, we would have to let him go and the whole thing would just start over again. Our only option was to kill him."

"And now, thanks to you," one of the other men said. "This melodrama is over."

"Wait," Jake suddenly interjected. "How did you guys get here?" He asked gesturing toward Roger and Connor. "I thought you had to have my family's DNA to time jump. Are you relatives too?"

"No," Roger answered. "Apparently Zander's theory about DNA and time travel was a load of bunk. Connor and I decided to try it while Zander was away, and we discovered that anybody can use the time machine."

"Yep," Connor said. "It turns out that it's the house that makes it all possible, not your DNA. We still haven't figured out why it works, though."

"I'm going to go get the old man," the boy said as he walked across the room to the time module, making sure to avoid the severed corpse on the floor. He turned the dials, grabbed the handles, and vanished in an instant.

"So, if Derek is dead for good," Jake asked the two remaining time travelers, "What about Zander. I'm pretty sure he's dead too."

"Yeah, but the kid will get him back," Roger answered.

"How is that possible?" Jake asked. "This time travel business is mind-boggling."

"Yeah, but you get used to it," Connor answered.

"The younger version of Zander has been living here in your time while his older self was working with you." Roger continued. "The old man staged him here to get him out of sticky situations he got himself into."

"Yeah, like when he got thrown in jail after attacking Derek at the police station," Connor laughed.

"Wait," Jake protested. "Zander told me that he set some automatic time jump thing that pulled him out of the jail cell."

Connor chuckled. "Yeah, well, he lied. What really happened is he called the kid when he was being booked into jail and the kid altered the timeline to get him out."

The time module clicked and whirred and both Zanders appeared. Old Zander surveyed the severed corpse on the floor and smiled. He looked up at Jake.

"Your handy work?" he asked.

"Unfortunately, yes," Jake answered.

"Nice job," Zander said, shaking his head. "Nice job indeed."

"So, what happens now?" Jake asked.

"We're going to clean this mess up and go back to our own time," Zander said. "I'll have to return my younger self to his appropriate time, of course, but everything should return to normal."

"What about Bridget's father?" Jake asked. "He was shot just before you."

"Oh, he's fine," Zander said. "Although, if he ever goes back to that wedding venue, he's going to have a vague deja vu experience of being shot there."

"So, that's it?" Jake asked. "We're done?"

"Pretty much," Zander answered. "Now you should go back to the wedding," he said, putting his hand on Jake's shoulder. "Tomorrow, everything will be back to normal."

Zander's departure was bittersweet for Jake. They had been through a lot together in the short time they had known each other. His assistants loaded Derek's remains into a large plastic bag and transported it to some other time. Zander left right after that with his younger self. Jake stood in the middle of the basement looking at the wall where the cabinet and the time module had been.

Suddenly and without warning, he found himself back at the wedding reception. Thomas and his new bride were having their first dance as a couple. As he stood watching the couple on the dance floor, Mia came up behind him.

"There you are," she said. "I've been looking all over for you."

"Oh," Jake mumbled. "Sorry. I didn't realize I was missing."

"Come on, let's hit the dance floor," Mia said, holding out her hand.

"I don't know," Jake said, hesitantly. "You know I'm not much of a dancer."

"Come on," Mia pleaded. "It's a slow dance."

Jake took her hand and walked onto the floor. As they danced, he looked around the room. The trauma he had just been through with Derek was still fresh in his mind, but nobody else seemed to have any memory of it. Bridget's father was sitting at a table talking to some people. Less than an hour earlier he had been shot dead by Derek. Jake marveled at how Zander could glide through time and undo the mayhem Derek had caused.

Thomas and Bridget danced their way across the dance floor to where Jake and Mia were slowly turning in circles.

"Hey bro," Thomas said in his usual cheery way. "We want you guys to come over tomorrow for a barbeque."

"Tomorrow?" Jake asked without thinking.

"Yeah," Thomas answered. "Before we leave on our honeymoon, we want to celebrate as a family, just us and you guys."

Jake was not answering fast enough, so Mia answered for them. "We'd love to come," she said.

The reception began winding down and Jake and Mia walked out to their car. Jake kept expecting to see Zander somewhere in the crowd, but he never did. As he and Mia drove home Jake wondered if he would ever see Zander again.

Chapter Thirteen

The aftermath

Jake awoke to his alarm at 5:30 A.M. He reached over and pushed the button to turn it off. He laid in bed for a few minutes trying to gather his thoughts. He wasn't completely sure what day it was. Thomas and Bridget's wedding was on Saturday so it must be Sunday. Why did his alarm go off?

He sat up in bed and looked around. He was not in his bedroom. He was in the master bedroom of the house on the corner. As he thought through the recent events and all the time traveling, he realized that the timeline must have changed. Did he own the house on the corner? If so, why couldn't he remember the events as they changed from what they were before?

He raised his arms above his head and stretched. His arms were sore and his right elbow hurt. He twisted his arm around to look at his elbow. It was bruised and scabbed over. 'The fight in the parking lot with Derek,' he thought to himself. 'This must be from the fight.' But young Zander had gone back and changed events so that Derek didn't attack at the wedding and Zander didn't get shot. Or maybe he just changed the events enough so that Zander and Bridget's father didn't get shot. Thinking about all the possible outcomes of time travel made his head hurt.

He got out of bed and staggered into the bathroom where Mia was putting on her makeup.

"Good morning, sleepy head," she said.

Jake sat on the edge of the bathtub. "What day is it?" he asked, yawning?

"It's Sunday."

"Then why did my alarm go off at 5:30? And why are you up so early?"

"I need to clean up the house before Thomas and his family come over this afternoon. I haven't done much cleaning lately with the wedding."

"Which was yesterday, right?" Jake asked, fishing for answers. He needed to find out what he had missed on this new timeline and how they had come to be in Thomas' old house.

Mia paused her makeup routine and looked at Jake. "Yes. It was yesterday. Are you sleep walking?"

Jake chuckled. "Maybe."

"You better get in the shower," Mia said, resuming her makeup application. "I'm going to need your help today."

Jake stood up and turned on the water to the shower.

"How long do you think we've been in this house?" He asked.

Mia turned and looked at him. "You're really not awake, are you? We just moved in here three months ago when Thomas and Bridget got engaged. Bridget already had a nice house, so Thomas decided it would be better to move there, rather than have her move into this house where he had lived with Janet."

"Right," Jake said through a yawn. "I think I'm waking up now." He raised his arms and stretched, pretending to still be half asleep. Mia noticed the bruise and scab on his arm.

"What happened to your arm?" she asked.

"Oh, I just hit it on something at the job site. It's fine."

Jake showered and got dressed. As usual, Mia had breakfast on the table when he came downstairs. He sat down at the table and loaded his plate with eggs, bacon, and toast. Mia sat across the table, watching him. Jake began eating before he noticed that she hadn't put anything on her plate. Then he noticed the smile on her face. "Aren't you going to eat?" He asked.

"Yes," she responded. "But before we eat, I have some news."

"What kind of news?" Jake asked, putting down his fork.

Mia couldn't contain her excitement. "We're going to have a baby," she squealed.

Jake stared at her in silence. He wasn't sure why he was surprised since Derek had claimed that she was pregnant. The fact that a time-traveling killer informed him of his wife's pregnancy before she did kind of ruined the moment.

"You're not excited," Mia said glumly, noticing the look on Jake's face.

"No," Jake protested. "I'm totally excited. I was just surprised, that's all. Congratulations!" He walked around the table and hugged her. "When are you due?"

"I don't know," she replied. "I'll have to make an appointment with the doctor to find out."

They spent the rest of the day cleaning; at least Mia did. Jake wandered around the house trying to get used to the new surroundings. He didn't recognize any of the furniture. It appeared to be new. He wondered what happened to the furniture they had at their old house, but he couldn't ask Mia about it. She would think he was losing his mind. Maybe he was.

The master bedroom was much larger than their previous home and had separate walk-in closets. He and Mia had shared a closet in their old house. He noticed that Mia's new closet was almost full of clothes and shoes, while his was half empty. He wondered how she could have filled it up so fast since she had doubled her closet space when they moved houses.

He walked into his closet and looked through his clothes. A shirt was falling off the hanger, so he pulled it out to re-hang it. As he put it back on the rod, he noticed the wood paneling on the wall behind his clothes looked like it was separating. He parted his clothes to look closer. He tried to push the panel back into place, but as he did, it swung open, revealing a secret compartment behind the wall.

The compartment was lined with shelves about a foot deep. Most of the shelves had stacks of papers on them. A few had some old guns and knives. On one end of the middle shelf there was a green military uniform folded neatly with a military hat on top. Jake pulled it out and looked at it. It appeared to be an authentic German uniform from one of the world wars.

He looked through the papers and found a letter addressed to George Holman. It read:

Dear Agent Holman,

On behalf of the British Empire and citizens around the world, I thank you for your exemplary service during our time of war. It's truly unfortunate that nobody will ever know of your heroic efforts to secure victory for the free world.

In order to provide for ongoing security for the device you recovered, £1,000,000 has been deposited into a Swiss bank account in your name. You will be able to access these funds to secure the device in your designated location in the U.S.

Please contact my office if you need further assistance. We wish you luck in your quest.

Yours truly,
C

Underneath the letter was a large envelope. Jake opened it and found a set of papers that looked like blueprints. The notations were written in a foreign language. At the top of the page there was a title:

Zeitmaschine

Jake pulled out his mobile phone and typed the word into the search bar. The information his search returned shocked him. Zeitmaschine was German for *Time Machine.*

The diagram on the page showed a series of turbines in a vertical position with a control panel in the middle. Jake searched for some of the other words on the page:

Der Weltraum – Space
Schwere – Gravity
Pordl -Portal

As he looked the document over, he realized that he was holding the blueprints and schematic for a time machine. But it didn't look like Zander's time machine. This device seemed to occupy an entire room. And why was it in German?

His thoughts were interrupted by Mia's voice calling him from downstairs.

"Jake, Thomas and Bridget are here."

He quickly folded the paper up, shoved it back in the envelope and put it back on the shelf. He closed the secret compartment and rearranged his clothes to cover it up. Then he rushed downstairs to meet his brother and his family.

Mia and Bridget were in the kitchen. Jake greeted them as he passed through to the backyard. Thomas was sitting in a lawn chair by the grill watching Tawny and Jeffrey play on the swing set.

"Sorry, Thomas," Jake said as he walked out to the patio. "I should have had the grill going. I guess I lost track of time."

"No problem," Thomas replied. "We're not in a hurry."

Jake lit the grill and went to the kitchen to grab the hamburger patties while it heated up. He carried the meat outside and placed it on the grill. Suddenly, he had a very strong Deja vu moment. This was just like the last barbeque they had together when Janet was poisoned, except now it was his house. He was grilling while Thomas sat in the lawn chair. Jake shuddered at the thought that this time Mia might be poisoned by some weird twist of fate. He shook the thought away and engaged in conversation with his brother.

"So, what did you guys do today?" Jake asked, trying to get a conversation started.

"The kids and I just visited Janet's grave this morning. We had a long talk about what cancer is and how their mother is in a better place now."

'Wait, what?' Jake thought to himself. Zander must have changed that timeline along with all the others he tampered with. Janet had died of cancer after all. How did he miss all of that?

"So, are Tawny and Jeffrey adjusting to everything okay?" Jake asked. "You know, with a new stepmom and house and everything?"

"Oh, yeah," Thomas said. "They love Bridget. She's really great with them. It really helped that she and her mom made sure the kids were super involved in the wedding. That made them feel really connected to her, you know?"

Jake couldn't hide his smile. 'Zander really did make things right,' he thought.

Bridget and Mia came out with potato salad and corn on the cobb. "Everybody ready to eat?" Bridget hollered, waving the kids over.

"Burgers are coming off the grill," Jake said.

The kids ran into the house and washed their hands. As everybody took their places around the patio table, Jake remembered the conversation they had at the last barbeque. Without thinking, he looked at the kids and said, "Did you guys ever go down in the basement when you lived here?"

Tawny looked at him and confidently said, "Yeah, all the time. Why?"

Jake was a little taken back by her answer, but he continued. "Well, your dad used to scare me with stories about a mummy in the basement."

Thomas put down his hamburger and stared at Jake with a perplexed look. "No, I didn't," he protested. "I would never scare you with stories like that. Why would you say that?"

Suddenly things were awkward. Jake wasn't sure what to say. He should have anticipated that absolutely everything was different now.

"Oh," he said, swallowing hard. "I guess my memory is not so good. Must have just been my childhood fear."

"Speaking of the basement," Thomas said, breaking the awkward silence. "I think I left some camping stuff down there in the cabinet. Can we go take a look?"

Jake nearly choked on his food. What cabinet? The only cabinet he remembered in the basement was the one with the time module. Was it back? If so, it might mean that Zander was close by. Then Jake's thought turned negative. 'What if the changes in the timeline brought Derek back?'

The thought worried him. Was somebody else going to die tonight, just like the last barbeque? Jake's mind was racing. How could he stop it? He started looking around for clues about who might be lurking nearby and what they might do. Thomas noticed his behavior.

"You all right, bro?" Thomas asked, his brow furrowed with concern.

Thomas' question snapped Jake out of his thoughts.

"Yeah," he answered. "I'm trying to remember what cabinet is in the basement."

"Oh, well, when we go down there, I'll show you," Thomas said.

Jake practically jumped out of his chair. "Let's go check it out."

"Now?" Thomas asked.

"Yeah, it will only take a minute."

"Can't that wait until we're done eating?" Mia begged.

"We'll be right back," Jake promised.

He snatched Mia's glass out of her hand as he walked past her toward the patio door at the back of the house. He poured her drink down the sink as he passed through the kitchen just to make sure she wasn't poisoned while he was gone. He was so wrapped up in his thoughts about time machines and murderers that he didn't even hear her object or the name she called him as he walked away with her drink.

"Okay, don't finish dinner, then." Bridget muttered as they walked into the house.

Jake felt his muscles tightening as he descended the steps to the basement. He marveled at how comfortable Thomas was compared to the last time they went down together. When they reached the bottom Jake peered into the room. He was relieved to see that the time module cabinet was not there, but there was a newer cabinet in its place. Thomas walked confidently across the floor toward it.

"This is the cabinet," he said, opening the door. "And here is the camping stuff I left in it." He pulled out a sleeping bag and a small tent and set them on the floor.

The brothers were about to go back upstairs when something caught Jake's eye. The old bookcase that sat against the far wall of the room appeared to have been moved. One side of it seemed to have become detached from the wall leaving a 6-inch gap on one side.

"Thomas, check this out," Jake said as he walked over to get a closer look.

"That's weird," Thomas said. "I thought this thing was attached to the wall."

Jake grabbed the edge of the bookcase and pulled it. It swung open like a door, revealing an opening in the wall. Jake glance back at Thomas, whose eyes were wide with surprise.

"No way," Thomas said as he gaped at the startling discovery.

Jake peered into the opening. It was pitch black. He couldn't see anything. He pulled out his mobile phone, turned on the flashlight app and shined it through the opening. He reached into the darkness and found a light switch. The light beyond the opening revealed a stairway that led down below the basement. Jake walked through the opening and looked down the stairs.

"What do you think is down there?" Thomas asked, poking his head through the opening to look down the stairs.

"I don't know," Jake answered. "Let's go down and find out."

"All this time our family has lived in this house, and nobody knew there was this secret room underneath the basement."

Jake descended the stairs, followed by Thomas. As the brothers reached the bottom, lights automatically came on, illuminating what appeared to be some kind of futuristic laboratory. The room at the bottom of the stairs was empty. On the opposite side of the room there was a door and a large observation window. Jake walked across the room and opened the door. The walls of the room on the other side were lined with large metal cylinders. In the center of the room there was a console with a milky glass top.

"What is all this stuff?" Thomas asked.

"I don't know."

"Kinda looks like Frankenstein's laboratory, doesn't it?"

"It looks futuristic to me."

Jake recognized the room from the blueprints he had found in the secret compartment in his closet. He walked around looking at the cylinders and examining the walls. The room was rectangular, slightly longer than it was wide. There was a cylinder in each corner and one in the center of each wall. One wall had a hatch in between the cylinders, like the door on a submarine, with a wheel to open and close it.

"I wonder what's behind this door?" Jake asked.

"I don't know."

Jake tried turning the wheel, but it wouldn't budge. He walked to the center of the room and sat down at the console. Suddenly, the glass top of the console lit up. A series of multi-colored lines appeared across the glass screen.

"What the heck is that thing?" Thomas asked nervously.

"I think it's some kind of computer."

As the machine clicked and whirred, a series of letters flashed across the screen:

Molecular **I**nter-dimensional **A**ccelerator

The words slid across the screen to the right and dissolved into three simple letters at the bottom right corner of the screen:

A series of digital dials and faders appeared in the glass screen. He recognized the dial in the center as the time destination selector, like the one Zander's machine had. There was a power switch in the upper left corner.

Without thinking things through, he reached over and tapped the power switch. The cylinders in the room began to hum. The sound was familiar. Jake had noticed it when he time jumped with Zander. He turned and looked at Thomas, who was standing in the doorway, obviously unnerved by the sound.

"What did you do, bro?" Thomas asked nervously as he backed slowly toward the stairs.

"I think I know what this is," Jake said.

Thomas didn't wait to hear more. "We gotta get out of here, man," he said, hysterically. "This thing sounds like it's going to blow." He scurried up the stairs and disappeared.

Jake turned back to the control board. His eye caught a digital throttle on the glass control panel that was labeled, *ENERGIZER*. As Jake looked at the throttle, it began to move forward on its own. The humming sound increased, and Jake felt the familiar sensations of time travel. The cylinders began to wind down and the humming sound stopped. He wasn't sure if he had really traveled through time. Nothing had changed in the room. He turned around in his chair and to his surprise, there was a man standing behind him.

"Hello, Jake," the mysterious man said in a British accent.

Jake lurched back and gasped, startled at the man's sudden presence. He recognized the man from the time fragment of the family at the dinner table he had seen.

"I'm sorry I startled you," the man continued. "I'm George Holman, and this is my time machine. And as a matter of fact, the house is mine as well."

"This is your time machine?" Jake asked. "That's interesting because I thought a man named Zander Knox built it."

"Oh, yes," George said sarcastically. "Zander Knox. The man from the future."

"So, you know him?" Jake asked.

"Oh yes, I know him," George said. "He's an idiot!"

Jake's jaw dropped in surprise. "Why do you say he's an idiot?"

"Well, what kind of a moron thinks you can travel through time using DNA? Knox's so-called time module simply tapped into the turbines here in this room. His contraption was simply an electromagnet that activated this inter-dimensional engine. In fact, he really has no idea how any of this works. He just, sort of, blundered into it."

Jake shifted his weight and scratched his head. He began to ask a question but then realized he had no idea what to ask.

"Time is a fourth dimension," George said, realizing that Jake was looking for an explanation. "In order to travel through it, you have to alter gravity to open up a wormhole. These gravity displacement turbines accomplish that. The wormhole allows you to move faster than the speed of light, which is ultimately how you travel through time. At least, that's the shortened version of it."

Jake stared at George in silence for a moment. His mind was totally blank. Finally, he blinked and took a deep breath. "I'm still a little unclear on who you are."

"Right," George replied. "As I said, I built this house about five years ago - you're in 1925, by the way – and this nifty time machine was installed several years ago. Coincidentally, the time travelers from the future arrived in my basement a few years before I got this thing working, which is rather interesting, don't you think?"

"Yeah, I guess," Jake said, scratching his forehead.

"As a matter of fact," George continued. "You were the first traveler to arrive in my basement, but you were dead at the time, so you probably don't remember.

"Anyway, your friends, Zander and Derek, really made a mess of things, jumping through time, killing people and so forth. Their random jumping created time fragments that made people think this house was haunted, which was actually quite a useful diversion, but I have spent considerable time putting things right."

"So, does Zander know that he didn't really invent time travel?"

George laughed. "No, he does not. In fact, right now he's trying to figure out why his so-called time module doesn't work anymore. He never has found this room, or even suspected it was here, which is surprising since he drew a chalk line around it on the basement floor above us. It never occurred to him that there might be something underneath his outline that was driving his so-called time module."

So, you disconnected his machine from this room?" Jake asked awkwardly.

"Yes," George said. "I can't have him going around messing things up anymore. I've worked hard to put things back the way they should be."

"All this time I thought Zander invented time travel," Jake said. "Then just today, I found the blueprints for this thing in a secret compartment in my closet. But the funny thing is that they were in German. It's also a very strange coincidence that I happened to find them on the same day that I met you."

"Well, it's really not a coincidence at all," George said. "I meant for you to find them. I can't run this thing forever. At some point I'll need to turn it over to someone else."

"Why can't you just shut it down?" Jake asked.

"Because the work I've been doing with it is too important," George said.

"What work is that?" Jake asked.

"I was a spy during the Great War, which in your time is known as World War One. We discovered that our enemy had plans to build a time machine. Apparently, some scientists from the future built one and someone went back in time to deliver the plans to our enemies. With a time machine, they could have altered the course of the war and secured their victory. We couldn't let that happen, so I was sent to steal the plans and destroy the machine.

"Once we had the plans and the device, we reconstructed it and a group of us transported some 300 years into the future and destroyed the original machine. At the end of the war, I was commissioned to take the plans and hide them here. The turbines and equipment we used to build our time machine were shipped here and I installed them in this room."

"So, after you destroyed the machine in the future, why didn't you just dismantle this one and be done with time travel?" Jake asked.

"Actually, we had to do a bit more than just destroy the time machine. We couldn't have anybody around who knew anything about it, so we had to deal with the scientists who built it.

"Anyway, now that time travel is possible, we have to safeguard it to make sure it's not used for ill-gotten purposes. That's what this machine is for, and the fewer people who know about it the better. I've gone to great lengths to keep this machine hidden, even fostering rumors about myself and my family to divert attention away from my real secret."

"So, what am I supposed to do?" Jake asked.

"For now, go back to your barbeque."

"That's it?"

"I'll be in touch soon. Until then, I don't want you to touch this machine. Is that clear?"

"Yep," Jake said. "By the way, why are there gaps in my memory? I woke up in this house this morning and apparently, I own it. I have no memory of that but everybody else does."

"Ah, yes. That's a little thing we call time slipping," George explained. "It's an irregularity of time travel that happens when you time jump and slip back into your timeline after the past has been changed."

"I see," Jake said, sarcastically. "I'll have to remember that term since it happens to me all the time."

"Right," George said with a wry smile.

"What's behind that door?" Jake asked, pointing to the metal door with the wheel handle.

"I will show you another time," George said. "For now, I want you to get back to your family dinner."

"How do I explain all of this?"

"You won't have to," George said. "When you get back, your family will think you just went to the bathroom."

"Okay, so what happens when I'm finished in the bathroom?" Jake asked with a smile.

"Oh, by the by," George interjected. "There is one problem that we're still trying to clear up, which I'll tell you more about later. And I probably shouldn't tell you this just now, but your wife, Mia, is not exactly who you think she is."

The comment shocked Jake. "What?" he stammered. "What do you mean?"

"I'll be in touch."

Before Jake could ask any more questions, George pulled a small remote control out of his pocket and punched some buttons.

"Goodbye, Jake. I'll be seeing you soon."

The turbines began humming and winding up like a jet engine. Soon, Jake felt the familiar falling feeling followed by weightlessness. The turbines wound down and he was back in his own time.

He climbed back up the stairs to the basement and pushed the bookshelf back into place. He climbed the stairs up to the ground floor and made his way to the backyard where his wife and Thomas' family were eating.

"Feeling better, Jake?" Thomas asked as Jake came outside.

"Yeah, I'm okay," Jake answered.

"Do you think it was something you ate?" Mia asked.

Jake eyed her with suspicion. "What are you talking about?" he asked, thinking only of the cryptic message George had dropped about his wife.

"Well, you jumped up and said, 'I gotta go to the bathroom' like it was some kind of emergency."

Jake realized that it wasn't the time or the place to confront his wife about what George had told him. "I'm fine now," he said at last, hoping to end the conversation.

After they finished eating Thomas joined his children playing frisbee. Jake had never seen him so active. Usually, he just watched his kids play. Now he was playing with them. He seemed like a different person.

That thought jarred him back to George's comment about Mia. What could he have possibly meant? Who was she? Was he safe being in the same house with her? Questions were swirling in his mind until Thomas and his family went home. When they were finally alone, he decided to confront her with the issue.

Mia was in the kitchen loading the dishwasher when Jake broached the subject. "So, how do you know George Holman?" He asked coyly.

Mia turned off the faucet and grabbed a towel to dry her hands. "Who?" she asked nervously.

"George Holman."

"You mean the guy who built this house?"

"Yes."

"Why would I know him?" Mia asked defiantly.

"That's what I'd like to know."

"Well, I know that he built this house," Mia said. "What are you getting at?"

"You know when I went to the bathroom during dinner?"

"Yeah?"

"I think you know I wasn't really in the bathroom."

"Where were you, then?" she asked innocently.

"I was down in the basement, talking to George Holman."

Mia's face turned pale, and she swallowed hard. "What did he say?"

"He said that you are not who I think you are."

Suddenly, Mia's demeanor turned to anger. "Argh," she bellowed. "That jerk. I told him not to say anything."

Chapter Fourteen

1917 – Rotterdam, Holland
Espionage

George Holman arrived at his office in Rotterdam, Holland at 8:00 am. The plaque on his office door identified him as a BBC News War Correspondent, but that was a cover identity. George Holman was a spy. His office was located down the hall from the Uranium Steamship Company. Before Europe became entangled in the Great War, the company offered low-cost transportation from the Netherlands to the United States for poor eastern European emigrants, but when the war broke out, it became a front for British espionage.

The neutrality of the Netherlands during World War One plus its location between England and Germany made it the perfect place for spies on both sides to set up stations. The German consulate, which was not far from the Uranium Steamship Company, was a hotbed of German espionage.

As George dropped his briefcase on this desk, he noticed a note from the MI6 station manager, who was known simply as "T". He wanted to see George in his office right away. George locked his door and walked down the hall to the Uranium Steamship offices.

"Good morning, Mr. Holman," the receptionist said as he walked through the door. "The director is anxious to see you. Please go right in."

T was a tall, thin man with a gaunt face and receding hairline. He usually wore a tweed suit with a bow tie. He was a serious man and rarely cracked a smile. He stood up when George walked into his office and extended his hand.

"George, thank you for coming so quickly. Please sit down," he said, gesturing to a chair near his large oak desk.

George silently took his seat and waited for the director to continue. T sat behind his desk and shuffled through some papers.

"We've received some intelligence that the Germans are working on – of all things – a time machine," T said. "Now, I don't believe it for a minute, but this information came from London, so I can't just disregard it, but I'm not sure how to proceed."

George chuckled. "Maybe the codebreakers deciphered something incorrectly. Where are they supposed to have this device?"

"Well, that's the interesting part of all this. Supposedly, they're building it in the German Consulate, just down the street from us."

"Well, that should be easy enough to check out," George said. "I think I can get in there and have a look around."

"How do you propose to do that?"

"The same way as last time when I verified that the consulate was being used for espionage."

"Good show," T replied. "Carry on, then. Let me know what you find."

George went back to his office where he had a German military uniform hidden in a locked filing cabinet. He changed into the uniform then taped a bandage on his throat. After checking his look in a mirror, he cautiously opened his office door and peered into the hallway. Finding the hallway empty he quickly closed his door and locked it.

He walked down the street to the German consulate. The guards saluted him as he entered the building. He presented himself at the security checkpoint and handed the officer his falsified credentials. The officer examined his papers and asked him a question in German. George pointed at the bandage on his neck and shook his head. The officer understood his motions.

"Wounded in battle?" the officer asked in German.

George nodded his head. The officer handed back the credentials and saluted. George returned the salute before turning and walking toward the stairwell. Although his military uniform got him through the front door, George didn't speak German very well. His accent would have given him away. The bandage on his throat allowed him to avoid speaking.

George's next step was risky. If the German's weren't working on a time machine he would be exposed. But his job was dangerous. He accepted that risk when he volunteered to leave his career as a reporter and engage in wartime espionage. He walked down the stairs to the basement and through the doors to a long hallway. He approached a soldier standing guard and held up a card that had one word: Zeitmaschine.

The guard read the card and pointed to a door about 50 feet down the hallway. George saluted and walked to the door. He put his hand on the doorknob, took a deep breath, and opened it. As he stepped inside, he found himself in the front office of a laboratory. Through a window on the far side of the room, he could see a group of scientists setting up an array of cylinders around the walls. One of the men in the front office approached him and spoke to him in German. He didn't understand what the man was saying, but it didn't matter. He pointed to the window and shook his fists in front of him as if to say, 'good job. Carry on."

George turned on his heels and walked back through the door to the hallway. He quickly walked back the way he came and exited the building through the front door. He picked up his pace as he walked down the street back to his office. After changing out of his uniform and back into his regular clothes, he hurried back to his supervisor's office. T rose from his desk as George burst through the door.

"Back so soon?" he asked.

George was too excited to sit down. He quickly rehearsed his escapade into the German spy headquarters. "I don't know if their machine will work," he concluded. "But they are definitely working on a time machine."

"Then we have to stop them," T responded. "As preposterous as it sounds, if they really can travel through time, they can change the course of the war, or the whole world for that matter."

T jumped up from his chair and strode across his large office to a cabinet. He unlocked the door and pulled out some blueprints, which he spread out across his desk.

"So, you say they have a laboratory set up here in the basement?" he said pointing to the plans on his desk.

"Yes," George said. He leaned in to get a better look at the plans, then pointed to a specific area. "Their lab is set up here."

T ran his finger across the plans as though he was tracing a route along the paper. As he got to the edge of the document he said, "There is an underground access to the basement here in the alley. It looks like it's accessible through the sewer tunnels. We need to put together a team to go in and destroy their machine."

"No," George interjected. "Let's seize their equipment and plans and set it up here in our station."

"Splendid idea," T said, pointing his index finger at George. "Let's put together a team straight away."

T opened his office door and called to his secretary. "Molly, please contact strike team one and have them report to my office at 15 hundred hours."

"Yes sir," she replied.

T slammed the door shut. "George, I want you to take the team and recover that equipment. I'll send an encoded telegram to London. We need to hit this tonight. There's no telling how far along they are with the machine or what it's capable of."

At 3:00 pm that afternoon, a group of six soldiers gathered in T's office to formulate a plan. George apprised them of the mission and showed them the blueprints of the German consulate. After discussing options for several hours, the team came up with a plan. The soldiers were dismissed to prepare, and George went home to have dinner with his family.

George was unusually quiet and pensive at dinner. He just picked at his food and didn't eat very much. His wife, Greta, noticed his mood.

"Is everything okay?" she asked as she began clearing the table. Josef and Annie had already taken their plates to the kitchen and had gone to their room.

"Yes, I'm fine," George answered. "I've just got a deadline at work I'm worried about. In fact, I'm going to have to go back to my office this evening to finish writing a story."

He hated lying to his wife, but he couldn't let her know what he was really doing. The less she knew of his activities the safer she and his children would be.

He met the commandos at a secret base at 9:00 pm. The team members were dressed in maintenance uniforms. They had acquired a large military transport to load the equipment in when they commandeered it from the German lab. The transport had been disguised to look like a utility truck. They hoped their cover as city maintenance workers would ease suspicions.

The soldiers drove to the back of the embassy and divided into teams of two. George had elected to walk to the embassy in order to determine if anybody might be watching. He took several diversions to throw off anybody who might be following him. When he was satisfied that he was alone, he met up with his team behind the embassy.

The advanced members of his team had already discovered the manhole cover that accessed the sewer tunnel. Two of them were waiting on the street level, while two of them had already gone underground to search for the access to the laboratory. George was escorted down into the tunnels, while two of the soldiers stayed above ground with the truck.

Using flashlights to light their way, George and his escorts found the advance soldiers not far from the access hole. They had found the door that led to the laboratory. The soldiers went ahead in case they met resistance. To their surprise there were no guards between them and the lab. George regrouped with the team at the door to the laboratory. The door was locked. Using a battering ram, the commandos breached the door and stormed the laboratory.

The German guards in the laboratory were not prepared for a breach from the tunnels and were taken completely by surprise. The three commandos quickly subdued them and tied them up. A few scientists were still in the laboratory. They surrendered without resistance. George began looking through the files and quickly found the schematics for the time machine. He walked into the room lined with cylinders and sat down at the control desk in the middle of the room. Referencing the schematics, he found a time selector and a lever labeled 'Energize.'

George turned the time selector knob to the right and pushed the lever forward to see what would happen. The cylinders began humming and suddenly George felt queasy. Then he felt very light, followed by the sensation that he was ripped off the floor and tossed across the room. Even though he hadn't moved, everything around him changed. He was in a different place.

*****

Jake was in his basement when he heard the turbines begin humming in the secret room below. It had been several weeks since he met George Holman. The basement began shaking. At first Jake thought it was an earthquake, but moments later, Zander appeared with his time module.

Zander let go of the handles and turned around. He smiled when he saw Jake. Before either could say a word, two German soldiers appeared. They were bound to chairs and gagged. Seconds later, George Holman appeared. He looked around, bewildered by his new surroundings.

"Where am I," he asked, looking at Jake.

"Hey George," Jake said. "Nice to see you again."

"How do you know me?" George asked.

"You time jumped here a few weeks ago."

"Did I," George said, with a smile. "Is this the future?"

"Yes," Jake answered.

"So, this thing really works."

"Wait," Jake said. "Is this the first time you've time traveled?"

"Yes," George said. "We just commandeered this machine from the Germans."

"This is weird," Jake said. "You built a time machine in this house. It's right underneath us."

"Really?" George said, somewhat bewildered. "You sound American. Where are we?"

"You're in America," Jake replied. "Last time you visited, you told me that you built this house in 1920 and installed the time machine a couple of years later."

"Huh," George mumbled, trying to grasp Jake's words. "Moments ago, we were in Rotterdam. Now we're in America. How is that possible?"

"Don't ask me," Jake said. "I'm a newbie with all this time travel stuff."

"As am I," George replied.

As suddenly as they appeared, George and the German soldiers disappeared leaving Zander and Jake alone in the basement. During the brief encounter, Zander had not uttered a word. He simply watched and listened as Jake and George talked. Jake turned to face

Zander whose head was slowly shaking back and forth as he looked at the floor.

"I have to admit," Zander said. "I'm a little confused about what's going on here. My machine suddenly stopped working. I've been working on it for weeks with no success. Then, all of a sudden, I'm transported back to your time."

"I hate to break the news," Jake said cautiously. "But it turns out that you didn't invent time travel."

Zander stared at Jake with a blank expression on his face.

"Apparently," Jake continued. "George Holman installed a time machine in a secret room underneath this room and your apparatus simply tapped into it."

Jake walked over to the bookcase and put his hand on it.

"After I saw you the last time, I discovered that this old bookcase was covering a hatch to a room below us. The real time machine is down there. In fact, I'm surprised to see you here because George said that he had disabled your time module."

"So that's why I haven't been able to get it to work?" Zander asked.

"It seems so," Jake replied.

"How did George manage to invent a time machine in 1920?"

"He didn't invent it," Jake quickly replied. "He told me that it was built by somebody way in the future and they went back in time to deliver the plans to the Germans in World War One. Apparently, George stole the time machine and reconstructed it under this house."

"So, if my time module has been disabled, how did I get here today?"

"No idea," Jake said, shaking his head.

Zander was silent for a moment as he considered the new reality. Finally, he sighed, and broke his silence. "Can I see the room down there?" he asked.

"Yeah, I guess," Jake answered. He pulled the bookcase toward him and walked through the opening to the top of the hidden stairwell. He descended the stairs, followed by Zander. Jake walked through the observation room and pulled the door open to the machine room. He entered the room and pointed out the cylinders lining the walls.

"Those turbines are what makes time travel possible. They create some kind of wormhole that you travel through. That's about all I know."

Zander walked around the room looking at the turbines and the control panel.

"So, the electromagnets on my machine just activated these turbines to open a wormhole?" Zander asked, mostly to himself.

"I guess so," Jake answered.

"I wonder how George disconnected me from it?"

"I have no idea."

"I wonder why he didn't talk to me?" Zander asked.

"I don't know. He seems to want to keep everyone from using time travel. He seemed kind of upset that you and Derek were using it."

Jake's comment annoyed Zander.

"As if he's the rights holder of time travel," Zander said, indignantly. "Knowing what I know now, I'll go back and secure the turbines and lock Holman out. He doesn't have the right to prevent me from having them…"

Zander and Jake looked at each other in silence for a moment. Finally, Zander spoke.

"Okay, I guess I'll go back to my time. Good to see you, Jake."

"You too," Jake replied.

The two men climbed back up the stairs to the basement above. Zander walked over to his time module and turned to face Jake.

"Until we meet again," Zander said, extending his hand.

"Do you really think we will?" Jake asked, shaking Zander's hand.

"You can count on it," Zander said.

He grabbed the handlebars and disappeared in an instant. Seconds later, the cabinet vanished as well.

*****

George and the German soldiers reappeared in the Rotterdam lab almost as quickly as they disappeared. The British commandos seized the soldiers just as soon as they arrived. They dragged the soldiers, still bound to their chairs, into the other room where they had secured the lab technicians.

George and his team quickly dismantled the equipment and loaded it into the truck. The captive soldiers and scientists were loaded into a paddy wagon to be transported to a cell in a secure government facility. As soon as they had the equipment loaded, George went back to the lab to make sure they had everything. He was worried that the Germans might have other copies of the plans and would be able to build another machine. As he was looking through filing cabinets an older man walked in through the front door. The man eyed George silently for a moment before he spoke.

"You're British," the man said with a heavy German accent.

"Yes," George answered nervously, wishing he had brought one of the commandos with him.

"Did you come for the machine?" the man asked calmly.

"Yes."

The scientist looked through the window into the other room and saw that all the equipment was gone.

"Did you get all the plans?"

"I don't know," George answered. "That's why I came back down."

The man glanced behind him, then locked the door. He walked briskly to a locked cabinet, pulled out a key and opened it. He withdrew a large envelope from the cabinet and closed the drawer.

"Here is a complete set of the plans in English," he said, handing the envelope to George. "You'll find the future coordinates of the machine builders in here. You'll need to neutralize them to prevent this machine from being used to change the outcome of the war."

George stared at the man in disbelief. "Why are you helping me?

"My colleagues and I are being held against our will. We're being forced to build this machine. If you're taking my companions, I want to come too. Without us, the Germans will not be able to complete this project."

"Okay," George said, nodding his head in understanding. "Your colleagues are already in a vehicle. Let's go."

George led the way through the tunnels and up the ladder to the alley where the commandos were waiting. When they saw Jake emerge with another man, they pointed their guns at him and ordered him to the ground. George quickly placed himself in between them to intervene.

"It's okay," he said. "He's here to help us. Please put your guns down."

The scientist disagreed. "No, please handcuff me. It needs to look like I was taken against my will in case somebody sees us."

One of the commandos stepped forward, placed him in cuffs and escorted him to the waiting vehicle. George climbed into the truck that had the equipment and they drove away. Once the equipment was stored in a secure location, George went to the Uranium Shipping office to report. T was standing behind his desk looking out the large window at the lights of the city. He turned around when George entered his office.

"Well?" He asked. "How did it go? Did you get the device?"

"Yes," George answered with a smile. "And it works. They actually had a working time machine, T. I accidentally transported myself to the future."

"Well, have they used it? Have they changed the course of the war? How would we know if they did?

"We have three of the scientists who worked on the project in custody. One of them seems to have overseen the program. He told me that they were being forced to work on the project against their will."

"Well done, George. We'll interrogate them first thing in the morning. For now, go home and get some rest. We have a busy day tomorrow."

*****

Zander arrived back in his lab and turned around to find his two assistants behind him.

"How long have I been gone?" He asked.

"Just a few minutes," Connor answered.

"How did you get it to work?" Roger asked.

"I didn't," Zander replied dejectedly. He explained how he had gone back in time and met Jake in the basement. "Turns out," he continued. "I've been wrong about pretty much everything. The real time machine is in a secret room directly underneath us. I guess the only thing I came up with was an electromagnet that activated the real time machine."

"What are you talking about?" Roger asked. "What's underneath us?"

Zander pointed to the old bookcase against the wall.

"Turns out," Zander said. "That old thing is hiding the access to a secret room that has the real time machine."

He walked over to the bookcase and pulled it open, revealing the access to the secret room.

"Come on, let's check it out," Zander said as he began descending the steps, followed by Roger and Conner. As they reached the bottom, the automatic lights illuminated the sub-basement rooms. Zander was completely dismayed to find the rooms completely empty.

"What's supposed to be down here?" Roger asked, surveying the empty room.

"All the equipment is gone," Zander replied. "When Jake showed me the room, it was full of equipment." Zander thought for a moment before continuing. "Maybe my machine works after all."

He rushed back up the stairs and strode over to the cabinet that contained his time module. He quickly turned the dial and grabbed the handlebars. Nothing happened. He shoved himself away from the module and cursed.

"What's the matter?" Connor asked.

"They removed the turbines. It looks like our time traveling days are over…for now."

Chapter Fifteen
The World War I Time Machine

George was in the interrogation room by 8:00 am the next morning. He sipped his cup of coffee while he waited for the prisoners to be brought in. T arrived next followed by the three scientists from the German lab. When the men were all seated, T sat down.

"Do any of you speak English?" he asked.

"We all speak English," one of the men answered.

"What's your name?" T asked.

"Dr. Klaus Muller," the man replied. "I am the lead scientist on the project."

"What can you tell us about the device you were working on?"

"It is a time machine, as you know. We were developing it to change the outcome of the war."

"Have you already used it for that purpose?"

"No," Klaus answered. "We had been given orders to change the outcome of the battle of Marne, but we had been stalling by telling them that the machine was not fully functional."

"Where did you get the plans for the machine?" George asked.

"They were delivered to us by the scientist who traveled back in time. As I told you last night, the packet I gave you has information about this. The thing you will find strange is that they were not German, they were Americans."

"Americans?" T exclaimed as he jumped out of his chair. "Why would American's want to change the course of the war?"

"That, they did not explain," Klaus said. "But my colleagues and I do not want the machine to be used this way. The Central Powers must not be allowed to win."

"We don't want it to be used that way either," T said.

"Dr. Muller," George said. "Can you help us reconstruct the machine in our facility?"

"Yes, as long as you will use it wisely. This technology must not be used to change the natural course of history."

"Agreed," T said. "Let's get it operational as soon as possible."

"Where do you want to set it up?" George asked.

"The Germans used their basement. We'll use ours," T said. "Make it happen, George," he said as he walked out the door.

"What do I do with the guards we captured?"

"Send them to a P.O.W. camp," he answered from the hallway.

George arranged to have a room cleared in the basement of the MI6 Rotterdam station. The equipment was delivered a short time later and the following morning, the German scientists began assembling it. While they worked, George looked over the documentation Dr. Muller had given him.

In addition to the plans for the time machine there was information about the scientists who developed it. One page had a graph that was labeled Coordinates. Below that were two subheadings, one labeled, Time Coordinates, and the other labeled Geo Coordinates. George recognized the geographic coordinates but couldn't understand the time graph. It had several vertical lines that bowed out, forming an arc. George walked over to where Dr. Muller was supervising the equipment installation.

"Dr. Muller?" George said, interrupting the scientist's discussion with one of his colleagues. "Can you help me understand what the graph on this page is?

Dr. Muller took the large page from George and set it on a table.

"These are time coordinates," He explained. "Instead of programming the day and year as we are accustomed to do with our calendar, the inventors from the future mapped their time and location as coordinates. This way we can program the machine to transport us to their precise location and time."

"Why can't they just list the calendar date?"

"Because calendars change over time. Thousands of years ago people used a lunar calendar. In our day we use a solar calendar. If we tried to go back 2000 years using our calendar, we would miss the mark because the calendars don't line up."

"So, what does this say about where and when they are?" George asked.

"They are more than 300 years in the future from our current time, and they are located in what is currently the United States according to these coordinates."

"Currently the United States?" George asked in surprise.

"Yes, the man who delivered these plans was from the American continent, but it may not be the United States in his time."

"So, this machine will, not only transport us through time, but also to another continent?"

"Yes," Dr. Muller replied. "Once you open up a wormhole, you can travel through time and to another physical destination."

"The machine is ready," said one of the lab techs, sitting at the control panel.

"Good," Dr. Muller said, turning to face the control panel. "Now we need to test it. Mr. Holman, are you willing to be a guinea pig?"

"Certainly," George answered. "I've already taken an accidental trip, which interestingly enough, was to the United States, now that I think of it. This time, let's stay a little closer to home, shall we?"

"Yes," Dr. Muller replied. "I have programmed the machine to take you to yesterday when you and the other man were interrogating me. When you are ready to jump, push this lever forward. The wormhole will place you just outside the conference room. You will observe our conversation for 30 seconds then jump back here."

"Got it," George said confidently.

Dr. Muller and the lab techs walked to an adjoining room where they could watch through a window. George sat down at the console, took a deep breath, and pushed the lever forward. Almost instantly, he found himself in the hallway outside the MI6 interrogation room just as T was walking out of the room.

"Send them to a P.O.W. camp," T said, looking over his shoulder. As he turned back in the direction he was walking he found George standing in front of him. "I just left you in the interrogation room. How did you get out here?"

"I'm time traveling," George answered as a wide smile formed on his face.

T took a few steps backward and peeked through the door to the interrogation room. George was sitting at the table with the scientist. He turned and looked back at George who was also standing in the hallway in front of him. Before T could say another word, George vanished.

Finding himself back in front of the time machine control console, George knew the test had been a success. Immediately the team of scientists burst through the door, followed by T.

"That was quite a stunt," T said as he approached the console.

"This thing really works," George said, excitedly.

"Apparently so," T replied.

"What do we do next?" George asked.

"Now you will need to neutralize the scientists who invented this machine," Dr. Muller said.

"What do you mean by 'neutralize'?" George asked, with a hint of suspicion in his voice.

"He means they must be killed," T replied.

George didn't like the idea of killing the scientists from the future, but he kept his feelings to himself. T organized a strike team to travel to the future with George. Once they had a plan, the group left for the day with plans to regroup the next morning to travel to the future and deal with the scientists.

George arrived home to the appetizing aroma of pea soup and sausage. Josef and Annie were already seated at the table and Greta was ladling soup into their bowls.

"Hi, Honey," Greta said as George came through the door. "Dinner is on the table."

"Smells wonderful," George said as he sat down. Greta ladled soup into his bowl before sitting down at the table.

"So how was school today? George asked his children.

"Okay," Josef answered glumly.

"We went on a fieldtrip," Annie said before slurping down a spoonful of soup.

"A fieldtrip?" George asked. "Where did you go?"

"We went to the zoo," she replied.

"Oh, what fun!" George said. "What was your favorite part?"

Before Annie could answer, there was a knock at the door.

"I wonder who that could be?" George asked, getting up from the table. He walked to the door and peeked through the peephole. He didn't recognize the man standing outside the door, so he didn't open it. If his role in espionage had been discovered, he and his family could be in danger. He couldn't risk that. He returned to the table and sat down to his dinner.

"Who was at the door?" Greta asked.

"Nobody," George said, hoping she would drop the subject.

"Well, it had to be somebody," Greta stated.

"I didn't recognize them, so I didn't open the door," George replied curtly.

"What if it's a neighbor who needs help?" Greta demanded.

"Okay, fine," George said, throwing his napkin down on the table as he pushed his chair back and rose to his feet. He trudged back to the door and looked through the peephole. The man was still there. He cautiously opened the door just enough to peek out.

A tall man with dark hair and a well-trimmed beard stood outside the door.

"Hello, George," the man said.

"I'm sorry," George replied. "Who are you?"

"My name is Derek Killian, and you are messing up my plans."

George was suddenly seized with fear. Could this be one of the scientists from the future?

"What plans might those be?" George asked, trying to remain calm. "And how do you know my name?"

"I'll explain all of that tomorrow when you visit me in my time," Derek said dryly. "Oh, and by the way, I've got your German scientists. What a disappointment they turned out to be." Derek turned to walk away. "I'll see you tomorrow about 300 years from now," he said, glancing over his shoulder.

George closed the door and locked it with trembling hands. He was totally unnerved by the mysterious man who clearly knew who he was and that he had a time machine. Was the man from the future playing a game with him? He couldn't help but wonder what would happen when he and his team traveled to the future. Was it a trap? Obviously, the mysterious man at his door knew his plans and was one step ahead of him.

He stumbled back to the dining room where his wife and two children had set their dinner aside and were waiting to find out who was at the door. George flopped down onto his chair.

"Are you okay?" Greta asked, noticing George's demeanor.

"I'm fine," George answered weakly.

"Who was at the door?"

"Oh, it was just somebody asking for directions," George lied.

"Then why are you so pale?" Greta demanded. "You look like you've seen a ghost!"

"I think maybe I have," George said, staring blankly at the table.

"Did you really see a ghost, Daddy?" Annie asked innocently.

"No," George replied. "That's just an expression when you see somebody that you haven't seen for a long time."

"So, it was somebody you know?" Greta asked.

"No, but there was something familiar about him. I just can't put my finger on it."

George debated on whether to call T and move up the expedition to the future or whether to wait until morning, when it was scheduled. As he considered the phenomenon of time travel, he realized that it didn't matter when they left, all that mattered was when they arrived. He decided to go to bed and take it up with T in the morning.

George arrived at the MI6 Rotterdam station at 8:00 am the next morning. The assault team was already there, armed, and ready. T arrived a few minutes later with the scientists. George was surprised to see them.

"T, I need to tell you something before we get started," George said.

"Can't it wait? We need to get this expedition under way immediately."

"No, it can't," George insisted. "A man from the future showed up at my door last night. They know we're coming, T."

The room went silent. All eyes were on George.

Dr. Muller stepped up to George and asked, "What did this man look like?"

"He was tall and thin with dark hair and a beard."

"This was the man who brought us the plans," Dr. Muller gasped.

"He also told me that he had you and the other scientists. Why would he say that?"

"I don't know," Dr. Muller said, shrugging his shoulders.

"So, what does all this mean?" T asked. "Do we need to scrap the mission?"

"I don't know," George replied. "They obviously know we're coming."

"We must complete the mission," Dr. Muller insisted.

His comment suddenly raised George's suspicion. Why was Dr. Muller so adamant about the mission? Why was he here when Derek Killian claimed he had taken them? 'Maybe Derek's comment didn't mean that he had kidnapped them,' George thought. 'Maybe he simply meant that they were on his side.'

"Why must we complete the mission, Dr. Muller?" George asked accusingly. "The man who came to my door last night said that he had you. Did he mean that you are really on his side?"

Dr. Muller's countenance fell. "No, I am not helping him," he said, fighting back tears. "He has taken my wife and child and is holding them prisoner in the future."

"Oh my," T gasped.

"He told me that I would get them back when I changed the course of the war."

"Hold on," George interjected. "I thought it was the Central Powers that wanted you to change the course of the battle of Marne."

"Yes, that is true," Dr. Muller said. "But it was I who brought the technology to them and convinced them that it could be done."

"What changed your mind?" T asked. "Why do you want to help us, when you know it will put your family in jeopardy?"

"Because it's the right thing to do. And I hope we can get my family back in the process."

"This Killian guy clearly knows we're coming," George said. "How can we regain the element of surprise?"

"I think I can help with that," one of the soldiers said, stepping forward. Addressing T, he asked, "if I may, sir."

"Please," T replied.

"I don't know much about time travel, the soldier said, "but I do know something about the element of surprise. We need to show up in the future when this Killian guy least expects us to be there."

"How do we know when that is?" T asked.

"Because the man from the future left time coordinates for us to follow," George said.

"Time coordinates?" T asked.

"Yes," Dr. Muller answered. "The man from the future left us his precise location in time so we would know how to reach him. He's expecting us to come at that time. But knowing when he expects us, we can alter our time and arrive before he expects us."

"It's a gamble," George admitted, "but it just might work."

"But you don't know what you're getting into so far in the future," T argued.

"No, we don't," George replied. "But what choice do we have?"

"I guess there is no other choice," T sighed. "Be careful."

"If something happens and I don't make it back…" George said.

"I will make sure your family is well taken care of," T said, finishing George's thought.

Dr. Muller staged the soldiers in the time machine and rehearsed the plan.

"We're going to send you to the future a few weeks before the future scientists have the machine working. We believe they will be in their lab with all the resources we need to secure. George will take the plans and the soldiers will take care of the people."

Dr. Muller handed a small metal box to George. The box had a button in the middle that was covered with a metal plate, which had to be flipped over to press the button.

"When you are ready to return," Dr. Muller explained. "Push this button. The wormhole will reopen, and you will be transported back to our facility."

Dr. Muller instructed George to sit at the console.

"When we leave the room, push this lever forward to initiate your time jump."

Dr. Muller left the room and closed the door behind him. He joined T and the other scientists who were watching through the window. George looked up at the commandos who were standing next to him.

"We have no idea what we will be jumping into," he said. "I think we need to be careful and not start shooting until we're sure of the target."

"Roger that!" the team leader replied.

George placed his hand on the lever. "Here we go," he said as he pushed it forward.

The group was immediately seized by the sensation of falling, followed by a feeling of weightlessness as the turbines interrupted the flow of gravity. Then they felt as though they were being pulled forward. Suddenly they found themselves in a different place. George looked around. The place looked familiar. He realized that they had been transported to the same basement he accidently transported to when they infiltrated the German lab. But now it was outfitted with an assortment of scientific equipment that was unlike anything George had ever seen.

The commandos readied their weapons and looked around the room. It was completely empty except for the equipment. The soldiers eased their grip on their guns and looked at George.

"Maybe we ended up in the wrong place," George shrugged.

Suddenly, a strange whirring sound caught their attention. They looked across the room to see a portal open. The dark-haired man with the beard stepped through it into the room. The soldiers immediately trained their weapons on him.

"Lower your weapons," he said, looking at the soldiers. He turned his gaze to George.

"I gotta hand it to you, George. I thought you would follow the time coordinates I left for you, but you were too smart to fall for that."

"Who are you?" George demanded.

"My name is Derek Killian," he said, turning his gaze to the soldiers who still had their weapons pointed at him. "I said you could lower your weapons," he said again.

"Permission to neutralize," the lead soldier called out to George.

"Granted," George replied.

The soldiers began shooting at the man but none of their bullets hit him. They seemed to go right through him. Derek stood still, smiling and shaking his head as the soldiers fired at him. Soon, the floor was littered with shell casings, but Derek was still standing, clearly unharmed by the barrage of firepower.

"I forgot to mention that I'm in another dimension," Derek teased with a wry smile. "Your bullets cannot hit me."

The soldiers lowered their weapons and looked toward George as if waiting for further instruction.

"So why did you want me to come here?" George asked. "And why did you say that you had the German scientists?"

"You're messing up my plans," Derek hissed angrily. "I've got a lot riding on the outcome of the war and you've jeopardized all that."

"You've got a time machine," George countered. "Why didn't you jump back in time and stop us?"

"Because you have an army," Derek replied. "And I am alone in my ambitions."

"What about the other scientists?" George asked.

"Oh, well, they don't help me much. You see, I keep them locked up unless I need something from them."

"You didn't invent this technology, then?" George asked.

"Of course not," Derek scoffed. "I just took control of it. The engineers who invented it are being held captive so they can continue to fine tune the technology. They have made me the most powerful person to have ever lived."

The soldiers rolled their eyes and raised their weapons at Derek.

"Say the word," the lead soldier said to George, "and we'll try to neutralize him again."

"Lower your weapons," George replied. "Clearly he has us at a disadvantage."

"That's an understatement," Derek gloated. "The only reason you're still alive is because I have chosen not to terminate you yet."

"And why haven't you terminated us?" George asked.

"There are things you need to do to bring about all this magnificent technology. I need you, George Holman. We're partners."

"We are not partners," George said, defiantly. You're a madman."

"No, I'm a clone," Derek replied with his head cocked to one side. "You probably don't know what that is, since you come from a primitive time, but in simple terms it means that I am a duplicate of the original Derek Killian.

"The original Killian stole a time machine and went around killing people. He became worried that something would happen to him so on one of his trips to the future he had a clone made – that's me – so that I could alter time and bring him back, if necessary. But once he was killed by your great great something grandson, I thought, why should I bring him back? I'm the most powerful being in the universe, why should I share my power with the original?"

Suddenly, a man in a white lab coat appeared through the portal holding a gun. He grabbed Derek by the throat and held the gun to his head.

"Give me my wife and daughter, or I'll pull the trigger."

"Dr. Muller," Derek said with a smile. "How nice to see you again. Your family is safe, and you may take them. I don't need you or them anymore."

Derek punched some buttons on his handheld device and a woman and child appeared next to George and the soldiers. Dr. Muller lowered his pistol and looked at his wife and daughter.

"Are you alright?" he asked.

"Of course, they're alright," Derek answered, mockingly. "You can clearly see they're fine."

"Did he hurt you?" Dr. Muller asked his wife, ignoring Derek.

"We just want to go home," she whispered, trying to hold back her tears.

"And home you shall go," Derek said, raising his handheld device. He punched a few buttons and Dr. Muller's wife and daughter disappeared.

"What did you do with them?" Dr. Muller demanded.

"Relax," Derek said. "I sent them back to your time. They'll be there when you get back. As for me, I've got some important things to do, so I will see you all soon."

Derek again pressed some buttons on his device and a dark opening appeared behind him. He turned and looked at the portal.

"Have you guys ever seen an inter-dimensional portal?" he asked as he gazed at the phenomenon behind him. "This portal will take me anywhere and any when I want to go."

Dr. Muller raised his gun toward Derek. "The only place you need to go is to hell."

Just as he pulled the trigger, Derek vanished into the black hole and the portal closed.

"Where did he go?" George asked.

"The machine will take him to any place and time," Dr. Muller answered. "It's impossible to know where he is now."

"How were you able to get to him when we couldn't?"

"This is not the first time I've traveled here," Dr. Muller explained. "I've been here many times trying to find my wife and son. I have observed Mr. Killian on many occasions, and I knew that he was able to manipulate time and space to be in multiple dimensions. I calculated this out after you left and that's how I managed to transport myself into his dimension."

"That would have been good information to have before we got here," George said with clear irritation. "The situation is different than we imagined, so what do we do now?"

"We need to see if the engineers are still here," Dr. Muller said. "If we can find them, we need to take them back with us."

George turned to the military team. "Search the place. See if you can find anybody here."

The soldiers trudged up the stairs, weapons ready.

"I'm going back to our time to see my family," Dr. Muller said. "I will talk to you when you come back." With that, he vanished into a time portal.

George followed the soldiers up the stairs to the main floor. As they went through every room, George realized that they were in a house that had been converted into a laboratory. Despite its Victorian architecture, the place had a slick futuristic feel to it.

The team went through every room in the building, but it was completely empty. They trudged back to the basement to decide what to do. George was ready to give up, thinking that Derek had somehow taken the engineers with him. While he conferred with the soldiers, he leaned on a bookcase against the wall. To his surprise, it moved against his weight. Upon further examination, he found that the bookcase was hiding an opening in the wall. Walking through the opening, he found the staircase that led to the room below the basement.

The soldiers went down first in case of danger. When they had determined it was safe, George went down. The room was filled with equipment very similar to the time machine George and his team had taken from the Germans.

"Does this stuff look familiar?" George asked his team.

Some of the men nodded and the team leader answered for them.

"Yeah, it looks like the machinery we took from the enemy in Rotterdam."

As George looked around the room, he noticed a metal door on one side with a rotary handle. He walked over and turned the handle, then pulled the door open, revealing a small holding cell. Two men and one young woman were being held there. One of the men was much older than the other two.

The prisoners were hesitant to come out, suspicious of the soldiers outside their cell.

"Are you alright?" George asked.

"We're being held here against our will," the older man said.

"Who are you?" the woman asked George.

"My name is George Holman. We came here from 1918."

The three prisoners exchanged glances and smiled.

"You are not with Derek Killian?" asked the younger man.

"No," George answered. "We came here to stop him."

The younger man stood up and walked to the door. "Then let's get out of here."

"What are your intentions with this time machine?" George demanded.

"Two of our colleagues are dead at the hands of Killian. He imprisoned us and forced us to work on the device. We never intended it to be used for evil."

"Well, you're free from Derek but if you want to stay free, you better come with us."

The three prisoners came out of the cell and looked suspiciously at the armed soldiers.

"Why do you have soldiers with you?" The older scientist asked.

"We came here to destroy this equipment. But the situation appears to be different than we thought. We are currently fighting a war in our time and Derek Killian brought this technology to our enemies with the intent of changing the course of the war. We seized their equipment and came here to destroy the machine you built."

"Then you had better destroy it," the woman said. "It has brought us nothing but misery."

"Yes," said the older scientist. "I regret building this machine. We never intended for it to be used to change the past. Now that Killian has the technology, he is extremely dangerous."

"If we destroy this equipment will that stop Derek?" George asked.

"I don't know," the older engineer answered. "Perhaps."

"Then let's blow this place up," George said.

"And take us with you," the woman said. "If we stay here, we're dead."

"Okay," George agreed. Turning to his military escorts he said, "Guys, light it up and let's go home."

The soldiers went to work placing explosives throughout the building, running fuses down to the basement. When they had everything in place, they lit the fuse and George pressed the button on his handheld device to transport them back to Rotterdam in 1918. As the group traveled through the wormhole back to their own time, the explosives they set off in the future lab could be heard and felt.

*****

T was surprised to see extra people in the group when they arrived back in Rotterdam. After giving an account of their experiences in the future, George introduced the engineers he brought back with him.

"I guess I never got your names," he said with some embarrassment.

"My name is Arthur Middleton," the older scientist volunteered. "This is Mia Andrews," he said, pointing to the woman. "And this," he paused. "This is George Henry Holman."

"George Holman?" T asked, looking back and forth between the George of the future and George, the spy.

"That's my name," the British spy objected.

"I was actually named after you," future George explained. "But I go by Henry. I'm your descendent."

"Fascinating," T exclaimed.

"How can that be?" the spy asked.

"Approximately two years from now," Henry explained, "you're going to build a house in America. That house will stay in the family until it becomes a research facility where we will successfully build a working time machine. Then as you know, that machine is taken by Derek Killian. And then you come with your commandos and blow the place up."

George the spy gasped.

"You blew up your own house?" T exclaimed.

"So, you knew I was coming today?" George asked.

"Yes," Arthur answered. "We didn't know specifically that it would be today, but we knew you were coming."

"By Jove, this time travel business is confusing," T said. "But apparently we know what to do now, thanks to these people."

Chapter Sixteen

Time Paradox

"So, what did George mean?" Jake demanded. "Who are you?" He was pressing his wife for answers after George Holman claimed that she was not who he thought she was. Mia clearly did not want to answer the question.

"I wish he hadn't told you that."

"But you obviously know him, or you wouldn't have called him a jerk for telling me there was something about you I didn't know."

"You called me a jerk?" said a voice behind them. Jake and Mia turned to find George standing behind them in their living room.

"George!" Jake exclaimed. "What are you doing here?"

"It's time we had a little chat," George said, ever the British agent.

"About what?" Jake asked.

"About time travel, obviously," Mia interjected in a sour tone.

Jake was astonished to hear her say the words.

"What do you know about time travel?" Jake asked without thinking.

"Quite a bit," George answered. "She invented it."

Jake's eyes darted back and forth between George and Mia as he tried to understand what was happening. "Is this some kind of joke?"

Mia looked at George. "I told you he wasn't going to take it well. That's why I'm upset that you told him before we were ready to explain things."

"Take what well?" Jake asked, defiantly, jumping up from the couch. "What's going on?"

George raised his hand and gently waved it up and down as he spoke.

"Now just calm down, Jake. Let me explain."

Jake sat back on the sofa. "I'm all ears," he sputtered.

"Your wife, Mia, is from the future. She was - or rather, will be - part of an engineering team that invents time travel."

"Why are you just telling me this now?" Jake demanded. "With all the time traveling mayhem that's been going on, why didn't you tell me this before?"

"Zander Knox's time traveling escapades were unexpected," George said. "He threw a wrench into our plans to be sure."

"What plans?"

"Things have gotten complicated," Mia said. "We need to start at the beginning, then we'll talk about the problem we have to deal with."

Jake sat silently eyeing George and Mia, waiting for one of them to continue. George began telling the story.

"As I told you before, I was a spy during the Great War. We received intelligence that the Germans were developing a time machine. I was sent to ascertain the reality of that. Once we confirmed it, we took it from them along with their engineers. We reconstructed the machine in our headquarters and jumped to the future to destroy the original machine and take care of the engineers that designed and built it. I think the actual word my superiors used was, 'neutralize,' which really meant that we were supposed to kill them. But when we arrived at the future, we found that the engineers had all been taken prisoner by a man named Derek Killian."

Jake sat straight up when he heard the name.

"Derek Killian," he exclaimed. "He's dead, though, right?

"Unfortunately, this isn't the Derek Killian you know," George answered. "He's a clone of the original man, and he's quite alive. He is, in fact, a deranged psychopath, I'm afraid."

"He killed two of our lead engineers on the project and locked us in the holding cell in the basement," Mia said. "He forced us to continue to work on the machine until it worked the way he wanted."

"Wait," Jake interjected. "Where did all this happen? Didn't this happen in the Netherlands?"

"No," George said. "The time machine was developed right here in the basement of this home."

Jake's head was spinning with confusion. "I thought you said that you built this house to hide the time machine that you brought from the Netherlands."

"Yes, that's correct," George answered. "As strange as it seems, the time machine that I hid downstairs was apparently still in the house when Mia and her colleagues found it and rebuilt it."

Jake took a deep breath and let out a sigh. "Wow," he exclaimed. "This is really hard to follow. So, what really came first?" He asked. "You built this house in 1920 and hid a time machine in it. Then, hundreds of years later, somebody builds the very same machine in the very same house. Is that what you're telling me?"

"Yes," George replied. "It's a bit of a paradox."

"So did they really build it or just restore it?" Jake asked.

"That's a difficult question to answer," Mia replied. "As George said, the whole situation is a paradox and it started with the research I did for my PhD. I designed a theoretical time machine that uses turbines to facilitate time dilation, which of course is the basis of time travel.

"One of my co-workers is a man named George Holman but he goes by, "Henry'. He's your direct descendent and he was actually named after this George right here. Henry and I were classmates at the university, and he would talk about this weird, old equipment in the basement of his home. A group of us became interested and Henry invited us over to look at it. When he took us down to the basement, I came face to face with the very turbines I designed for my PhD.

"When I saw that," Mia continued. "I knew that time travel was possible and that somehow, I had already invented it. The question nobody can answer is, 'how could the machine that I designed for my PhD already exist?'

"Right," George interjected. "My theory is that an alternate version of Mia invented it and it got caught in a time loop of some kind."

"Anyway," Mia said, regaining control of the story. "A group of us started working on the machine. In addition to myself and Henry, an electrical engineer named Arthur Middleton and two mechanical engineers were invited to work on the machine.

"It was an exciting time. We managed to get the machine working and made some significant improvements. Then Derek showed up. He made demands of us that we didn't want to do, so to motivate us, he vaporized the mechanical engineers. He locked the rest of us in the holding cell downstairs to prevent us from leaving."

"Wait a minute," Jake said, remembering the metal door in the sub-basement. "So, behind the metal door is a prison cell?"

"When I built the house," George said, "The door opened to a tunnel that led to an access point on the other side of the property. The generator that powers the machine is also down there."

"The generator was Arthur's contribution to the project," Mia interjected. "The machine has substantial power requirements that can't be accommodated with the main power grid."

"When Derek hijacked the project," George said, "He blocked off the tunnel and created a holding cell that he could isolate the engineers in."

Turning to Mia, Jake said, "So, obviously you've known about the machine in the basement this whole time."

Mia looked away and nodded. Jake could see tears welling up in her eyes as her secrets were all on the table.

"And you knew who Zander Knox really was?"

Mia silently nodded again.

"So the day that I came home and told you that Janet was back, and we went over, and weird stuff happened…you knew exactly what was happening the whole time?"

"Yes," Mia squeaked as she nodded her head.

"I feel like a total dimwit for not seeing this," Jake said. "You led me to believe that you grew up here, went to school here, got a teaching degree and were a schoolteacher."

"I did grow up here," Mia insisted, "and I am a schoolteacher now, but I grew up hundreds of years from now and my original degree was in quantum physics."

"In fact," George interjected. "She graduated the university with her degree when she was just 18 years old."

"Well, I'd say you are a little overqualified to be teaching elementary school," Jake said, sarcastically.

"That's a good point," George interjected, "I'm glad you brought that up. After we rescued the engineers from the future, we staged them at different coordinates on the timeline to watch for Derek Killian's clone. Mia was assigned to your time. Her mission was to live here near the house and watch for Derek. She alerted me immediately when he poisoned your sister-in-law, but that twit, Zander, was meddling with the timeline, and we had to be careful. When Derek didn't recognize Mia, we knew that it was the original Derek and not the clone.

"With Mia being stationed in your time, she needed a way to blend in and since her physics knowledge was 300 years more advanced than what your generation currently knows, it didn't make sense for her to get a job in physics or teach at a university level. It would be difficult for her to keep her advanced knowledge from being shared with the scientific community that isn't ready for it, so she opted to teach elementary school."

"I love my life now," Mia insisted. She leaned forward to face Jake. "And I love you. The best thing that ever happened to me was meeting you."

"But it was just part of the plan, right?" Jake sneered.

"Not at all," George replied. "The plan was for her to get to know you, not to fall in love with you."

"That makes me feel so much better," Jake mumbled sarcastically. "Why did you wait until now to tell me all of this?"

George answered the question. "Because Mia was afraid to tell you the truth. In fact, she didn't want you to ever know. And if you hadn't been dragged into the mess that Zander created, you would never have known about any of this. It's taken me a while to convince her that we need to bring you in on the secret. I decided to give the subject a nudge when I spoke to you downstairs. Sadly, she's concerned that this information might damage your marriage."

Jake looked up at Mia. She was looking at the floor, wiping tears from her eyes. Jake was feeling a range of emotions. He was angry that Mia kept the truth from him. Finding out that she was a genius made him feel inferior. Knowing that she pretended to be clueless when she really knew more about the situation than he did made him feel stupid.

"I can't believe this is happening," he said. "I wish we could go back to the way things were before all this time travel stuff happened."

"So do I," Mia said softly.

"Unfortunately, that's not an option," George said. "Time travel has been a part of your life since you were born. You grew up in this house that was built with a time machine in the basement. People have been time traveling through here your entire life."

"Fair enough," Jake said glumly. "So, what's this plan you were talking about?"

"We have to catch a deranged psychopath," George said. "Derek Killian's clone has the most advanced and powerful time machine imaginable. In order for us to catch him, we're going to have to upgrade the device in the basement. We can't do that, 'under the radar,' so to speak, so you need to know what's going on."

"Why does it have to be done in my time? Why couldn't you upgrade the machine in your time?"

"Because Mia refuses to be away from you and she's the lead engineer. It's her project."

George's statement caused Jake to feel a rush of emotion. He looked up at Mia, who was looking back at him with tears in her eyes. He was beginning to appreciate that she gave up her future to be with him. And he had so much more to learn about her – things that she had not been able to tell him before.

The sound of George's voice brought Jake out of his thoughts.

"We're going to need the other two engineers on the project as well, so they're going to need to live here for a while. Is that alright?"

"What?" Jake asked before George's words sunk in. "Why can't they just stay in their assigned time and time travel in to work?"

"I suppose that will work," George replied with a wry smile.

George noticed how Jake and Mia were looking at each other and realized it was time for him to leave. He would be back with the other project engineers to begin work on the upgrades for the time machine. For now, the couple needed some time to themselves.

"I think it's time for me to take my leave," George said, rising from the couch.

Jake stood up out of courtesy and habit.

"Don't get up," George protested. "I know my way out."

Jake walked over to Mia, took her hands and raised her from her chair. He wrapped his arms around her in a tight embrace.

"I guess I don't really know very much about you," he said. "I'm looking forward to getting to know you all over again."

As he held his wife close, he realized that life as he had known it was at an end. His new life would forever include time travel, and consequently, a cunning clone, who just didn't seem to go away.

He was about to embark on two new adventures: one to find a madman, and one to get to know his wife all over again. This time it would be the real Mia.

Chapter Seventeen

Unexpected Revelations

"Are we safe living in this house with a mad man on the loose?" Jake asked. He found it difficult to ask his wife questions about time travel, even though he knew that she invented it.

"We should be safe," Mia replied. "We've installed disrupter panels around the house to prevent anyone from time traveling into our home. If and when *we* use the machine, we'll turn them off, but they should prevent the clone from getting into our house through a time portal."

Jake and Mia were sitting on the back porch on a Sunday morning, enjoying the cool air on a sunny spring day.

"You know," Jake said. "It's a little intimidating to realize that you're this genius scientist from the future."

Mia sat in silence for a moment before answering. "I don't know why you would say that," she began. "I'm the same person you've been married to for nearly four years."

"No," Jake protested. "The woman I married and the woman you turned out to be are two completely different people."

"Not true," Mia countered. "I'm exactly the same person you married. You just didn't know that I had a Ph.D. in quantum physics…300 years from now."

"Yeah, that's the part that intimidates me."

"Well, get over it," Mia said unapologetically. "We have a psychopath to catch."

"Yeah, about that…so, he's a clone?"

"Apparently."

"You never met the original Derek?"

"The one you eliminated? No."

"Yeah, well, first, I was just trying to prevent him from escaping. And second, what if that one wasn't the real Derek, either?"

Mia thought about the question before answering. "Well," she said at last. "That could be bad. All we can do at this point is focus on the one we know of and try to stop him."

The couple sat in silence for a few minutes before Jake asked another question.

"Do you miss your life in the future?" he asked hesitantly.

"Some things I miss," she answered. "Some things I don't. And I definitely wouldn't trade it for my life here and now with you."

"Wow," Jake said. "That makes me feel really good. Would you want to go to your time in the future and visit?"

"Well," Mia replied contemplatively. "I don't think that would be a good idea. The time machine we built in the future was destroyed. I'm afraid going forward to that time would complicate things."

"How so?"

"I don't know," Mia answered. "What if we somehow changed things and brought the time machine back? I don't think we should risk that."

"Don't you miss your family?"

Tears welled up in Mia's eyes as she contemplated the question. "I don't have any family there anymore."

Jake didn't know how to respond. He wanted to ask about her family, but he could tell it was a touchy subject. After a few minutes of silently rocking on the swing, Mia shared more of the story.

"The two engineers that Derek killed were my parents. I was an only child."

"I'm so sorry," Jake gasped.

A few more minutes of silence passed as the couple rocked back and forth in the porch swing. Jake's mind was swirling with questions about time travel and how it played into recent events. Finally, he broke the silence.

"Can I ask you some questions about time travel?

"Sure," Mia replied.

"When Zander first showed up," Jake began. "He seemed to be able to transform the whole house through time travel, but later he told me that the time machine only transported you if you were within the lines he drew on the floor. He also time jumped out of jail after he assaulted Derek. How does all that work if you have to be inside the machine to time jump?"

Mia smiled as she contemplated her answer. "First of all, Zander is not the most brilliant scientist on the planet. The only thing he invented was a device that activated the machine that my team and I built 150 years later. Second, he had his younger version operating the machine at the time, and third, it's not really a time machine, it's a molecular inter-dimensional accelerator. It opens a portal that allows you to travel to any place and time in the universe as long as you have the coordinates to get there."

Jake remembered seeing the words, **M**olecular **I**nter-Dimensional **A**ccelerator on the computer screen of the time machine, before it dissolved into the acronym, MIA. "So, you named the machine after yourself?" He asked.

"That's another part of the paradox," Mia replied." Did I name the machine after myself, or was I named after it? We don't know the answer."

Jake was silent for a few moments before asking his next question.

"Why did it cut Derek in half?"

"Because when Derek straddled the line, half his body began moving faster than the other half, so when the turbines got up to full speed, half of him moved at the speed of light and the other half didn't, so in reality, it actually *tore* him in half rather than *cut* him in half."

The couple rocked back and forth in silence for a few minutes before Jake asked his next question. "So, when are we going to talk about this plan that George mentioned?"

"I don't know," Mia answered with a sigh. "There's something about all this I haven't brought up with him yet. I haven't been able to figure out the best way to bring it up. It's kind of an awkward situation."

"Why is it awkward? Why can't you just tell him whatever it is that you need to tell him?"

"Don't you think it's weird that George has never questioned why Derek wanted to sway the outcome of World War I?" Mia asked, cutting into Jake's question.

"I've never thought about it. What are you getting at?"

"Did you know that George's wife is German?"

"No, I didn't know that."

"Did you know that she was part of the German royal family?"

"I didn't know there was a German royal family."

"Well, there was until the end of World War I. When Germany lost the war, they were exiled to the Netherlands."

"So, what are you saying?" Jake pressed. "Did George's wife have something to do with the German's getting the time machine?"

"Yes, that's exactly what I'm saying."

"Wow," Jake gasped. "You don't think he knows that?"

"I don't know what he knows. He's never brought it up. He's never once asked if we know why Derek wanted Germany to have the technology."

"How do you know that George's wife was involved?" Jake asked.

"I don't know for sure," Mia answered. "But Derek told us that he was doing this for a member of the royal family who had promised him a fortune if he helped the Kaiser stay in power."

"Why do you think it was George's wife and not another member of the royal family?"

"Because he mentioned her by name; Greta Holman."

"Are you sure?" Jake inquired.

"I'm positive," Mia answered confidently. "Henry, Arthur and I talked about it a lot while we worked on the project and while we were locked in the holding cell. The clone was pretty clear about who she was."

"I can see why you haven't wanted to bring it up," Jake admitted. "Do you think that George knows, and he just wants to silence Derek?"

"I've thought about that, but either way, Derek is dangerous."

"Yes, but can we trust George Holman?"

"So far he's never given me a reason not to trust him."

"Well, at some point, I guess we'll find out."

Chapter Eighteen

The plan

The team was gathered in the living room of the house on the corner to discuss the plan to catch Derek. The team consisted of George Holman from the past, George Henry Holman from the future, Jake, Mia, and Arthur Middleton. Arthur was the oldest member of the group. He was a crusty old engineer who didn't hesitate to speak his mind, even when nobody was interested in his opinion. He was also the only person in the group who had not owned the home at one time. In the present time, the home belonged to Jake and Mia, but that didn't prevent George and Henry from referring to the home as "my home".

Everyone but Jake was already aware of the basic plan since it had been formulated in his absence before they decided to bring him into their confidence. The plan was to lure Derek into the time machine, then trap him in a time loop. The team was engaged in a lively debate about how to accomplish this and Jake felt completely lost by their technical jargon. He caught words and phrases like inter-dimensional portal, gravity displacement, biomarkers and age-related measurements. Finally, he got up and walked into the kitchen to get a drink.

"Hey, where do you think you're going?" Arthur Middleton growled as Jake made his exit.

Arthur's gruff question brought the discussion to a halt, but Jake ignored him. He grabbed a glass, filled it with water and sat down at the table. Soon, Mia came and sat down beside him. "Are you okay?" She asked.

"I'm fine," Jake said glumly. "I'm clearly not needed in there," he said, nodding toward the living room.

"But I want you to be a part of this. You need to know what's going on," Mia said.

"I only understand about one out of every four words," Jake retorted. "This stuff is all way over my head."

That's okay, Jake ol' boy," George Holman said, strolling into the kitchen. "I don't understand much of it either. Why don't you come back in and we'll have these eggheads try to explain it in simple terms."

"Naw, I'm good," Jake said, shaking his head. "The only reason you're having these meetings in my time is because Mia insisted."

"That's not entirely true," George said. "We do need you, but I've hesitated stating the reason why." George said.

Jake gazed at the British man expectantly. George looked over his shoulder to see if anyone was behind him, then leaned in closer to Jake.

"We need somebody who can fight," he whispered. "The brilliant minds in the other room are all brains and no brawn. They're total marshmallows."

Jake looked at Mia who returned his gaze with a smile. "I think you're just saying that to make me feel better," he said.

"No, I'm dead serious," George assured him. "If Derek comes out fighting, what are these guys going to do? Beat him with their slide rules?"

Mia laughed. "Slide rules are from your ancient time, not ours."

Jake looked at Mia and George momentarily before asking, "What's a slide rule?"

Mia just laughed and gestured to George to answer.

"Back in the good old days," George began. "Back before calculators and computers and such, we used a sort of, mechanical analog computer to make mathematical calculations. It was like a ruler with a slider in the middle. It was really quite useful back in the day."

The banter lightened Jake's mood and he chuckled at the thought of scientists in lab coats fighting with slide rules.

"Why don't you come back to the other room and let us bring you up to speed?" George pleaded.

"Simple words!" Jake insisted as he stood up and walked toward the living room.

Arthur couldn't help making a snide remark as Jake came back into the room. "Alright, soldier, sit down and let us dumb this down for you," Arthur growled.

Jake pointed his finger at the older man and said, "Shut it old man or I'll pick you up and throw you out of my house."

The room went silent. Nobody had heard this kind of outburst from Jake. Mia took it as a signal that her husband was really on edge. George and Henry couldn't let the remark go without pointing out that they, too, were owners of the house.

"Yeah," Jake said smugly. "Well, right now in this time, the house is mine. If you want to move to another time dimension when you actually occupied the house be my guest. But here and now, it's my house, so be nice or get out!"

His firm statement was met with silence. Finally, George broke it. "Right then, let's get on with it shall we? And Arthur, be nice."

The older man leaned back in his chair and rolled his eyes.

"Mia," George continued. "Would you start our discussion with an overview of the current situation with the clone?"

"Okay," Mia began. "Just before the time machine in the future was blown up, Derek, the clone, escaped into an inter-dimensional portal, which for the sake of brevity, we'll call a wormhole. We think that he might be trapped in it because the machine he used to get to it was destroyed. In theory, in order for him to get back here, he needs a machine with the same capabilities as the one we built."

"So, your machine is different than this one?" Jake asked.

"It has some capabilities that this one doesn't," Mia replied.

"Keep in mind that this is all theoretical at this point," Henry interjected. "We don't know for sure what happened to the clone after we blew the system. He could be dead for all we know."

"He's not dead," Arthur grumbled. "You know that!"

"Anyway," Mia continued. "The idea we're discussing is to modify the machine so that he can come out of the portal and back into the machine. If we can get him back into the time machine, we can trap him in a time loop to age him quickly and hopefully, he'll just fade away."

"Why would he age quickly if he's caught in a time loop?" Jake asked.

"Well, normally he wouldn't..." Mia began.

"But we're talking about a microgravity time loop," Henry interrupted excitedly. "The lack of gravity in the time loop will accelerate all biomarker-measured, age-related aspects of the clone. The only question is how long it will take for him to die."

"You used a lot of big terms," Jake protested. "I thought we were going to keep it simple."

"In simple terms," Arthur sneered, "We're going to kill the clone using artificially created natural causes...so to speak."

"We've already figured out the time loop part of the plan," Mia continued. "Before we go to that effort, we want to see if we can verify that Derek is really trapped in the wormhole and where he currently is in the time spectrum."

"That's where I come in," Arthur said. "I've already designed the tracking device that will allow us to look into the wormhole. We can program a DNA sample into it and track Derek no matter where he is. The next step is to build it."

"And now you know everything we know," George exclaimed. "So, let's get to work."

Henry and Arthur went downstairs to begin work on the tracking device. George, Mia and Jake remained upstairs. Mia had decided to talk to George about his wife's possible connection to Derek, but she was not sure how to bring it up. Jake saved her the trouble and blurted out a question without thinking.

"Why do you think Derek wanted the Germans to have the time machine?" Jake asked after the two scientists left.

"He wanted to change the outcome of the war," George replied.

"Yes, but why would he care? He was born hundreds of years after the war."

"Ah," George exclaimed, realizing where the conversation was going. "You think my wife put him up to it."

"You know about that?" Mia gasped.

"Of course, I know about it. I'm a spy."

"But you've never mentioned it, so I thought maybe you didn't know."

"Things are not always what they seem," George replied. "Derek had been traveling through time, experiencing historical events first-hand. He had a random chance encounter with my wife in a park in Rotterdam.

"Greta was sitting on a park bench, watching our children play when Derek came and sat on the bench next to her. In the course of their conversation, Derek realized that she was German. He told her that he had a time machine and had traveled from the future and that Germany would lose the war.

"She, of course, thought he was joking, so she replied with something like, 'oh really? Well, I'm the Kaiser's daughter. If you have a time machine, then you can change the course of the war so my family can stay in power.

"Derek, deranged as he was, took her seriously and struck a bargain with her to be handsomely compensated for doing so. My wife agreed, of course, thinking that he was in jest."

"So, your wife is not really the Kaiser's daughter?" Jake asked.

"Heavens no," George chuckled. "She's never even met the royal family."

"Why didn't you tell us this before?" Mia asked.

"I didn't realize it was an issue."

Mia breathed a sigh of relief. "Derek was always spouting off about how he was helping the daughter of the Kaiser keep her family in power. He had me totally believing your wife was behind all of it."

"You could have Googled it," George chuckled. "Or don't they have Google in your time?"

Mia responded by rolling her eyes.

"I've actually found the Internet quite helpful," George continued. "I wish we had it in my day, but as you know, I can always jump forward and use Jake's computer."

"I don't have a computer," Jake sputtered. "The computer in the house is Mia's. I'm just the dumb guy with a smartphone."

"But of course, you can use it to Google stuff anytime you like," Mia said sarcastically.

"Well, now that we've put that nasty rumor to bed, let's get on with our work, shall we?" George said, rising from his chair.

"Yeah, I've got to get to work," Jake said. He kissed his wife and walked out the door.

Mia had resigned her position as a schoolteacher to focus on the upgrades they were making on the time machine. She never needed the money. One of the advantages of coming back from the future is knowing what happens to money markets. The three scientists had leveraged this to their advantage and were able to live off the investments they had made. While she missed teaching, she enjoyed physics much more.

Chapter Nineteen

A Clone Encounter

Jake was relieved to be going to work. He was not comfortable around the group of scientists from the future. He was still getting used to being married to one of them. He felt a lot more comfortable when he thought that his wife was a schoolteacher instead of a genius-level physicist from the future. When he would hear her talking with her colleagues, it was almost like she was speaking a different language.

George Holman seemed to fit into the group of scientists with ease, but Jake felt like an outsider. George had tried to reassure him that he was a necessary part of the group, but Jake doubted his sincerity. He suspected that George was just trying to assuage the situation to keep Mia happy. And after hearing their plan to capture Derek Killian's clone, Jake didn't see how any of it would involve him. But that was about to change.

He pulled up to his job site and climbed down out of his truck. As he walked toward the construction zone, he was met by the job foreman.

"Some guy has been waiting here to see you for about an hour. He's over there in the office."

"Who is he?" Jake asked.

"I don't know," the foreman answered. "Wouldn't say who he is or what he wanted. But he's sort of creepy."

Jake walked toward the construction office, his heart beating faster with each step. By the time he reached the door, his heart felt like it was pounding in his chest. He tried to calm himself before he opened the door, tried telling himself that he was getting worked up over nothing. But in order to calm his fears, he knew he would have to open the door and find out who was on the other side. The door swung open and confirmed his worst fear: Derek Killian was waiting for him inside.

Jake wasn't sure if it was the clone or the real Derek Killian he had killed. With time travel, anything seemed possible. But this version of Derek, whoever he was, did not look well. His face had a pallid complexion and he looked haggard and worn. He looked considerably older than the previous version he had seen. His breathing was raspy and labored.

"I'm guessing you're Jake," the man said feebly.

"And you must be the clone," Jake answered.

"If by clone you mean a better and smarter version of the original, then yes, I'm a clone."

"That's funny," Jake said. "Because you don't look better than the original. You look like you're nearly dead."

The clone coughed. "The consequences of being trapped in an inter-dimensional portal, I suppose."

"How did you get out?" Jake asked warily.

"Like I told you. I'm an improved version of my original. That means I'm smarter than he was."

"Whatever that means," Jake muttered.

"All right," the clone snapped. "Let's cut to the chase. I need the time machine you've got locked up in your basement."

"Oh," Jake said with pretended sympathy. "What's the matter?" he continued, mockingly. "Can't get to the original one in the future? Oh, that's right, it got blown up."

The clone coughed again. "A minor oversight on my part," the clone wheezed. "I didn't realize they were intent on destroying it."

"You better get that cough looked at," Jake mocked. "That doesn't sound good."

"That's why I need the machine," Derek snapped. "I need to go forward to the time I was cloned. Turns out that clones don't live as long as the originals. And being trapped in a wormhole accelerated some aging aspects that I wasn't anticipating, so I need the cloning technology to recondition myself."

"Yeah, that's not happening," Jake said.

"Oh, I think it is," the clone replied smugly. "Because I've got a little insurance policy to make sure it does. I've got your brother and his family."

Jake felt a shockwave course through his body. Could it be true? Was Derek bluffing? "I don't believe you," Jake replied.

"Try calling your brother."

Jake pulled his phone out of his pocket and called Thomas. The phone Derek was holding started ringing. Smugly, the clone punched a button on the phone and raised it to his ear. "Hello, Thomas can't come to the phone right now, because he's been kidnapped."

Jake disconnected the call and shoved the phone into his pocket. "That doesn't prove anything," he protested. "Phones are easily hacked."

"Yeah, I know," The clone said smugly. "But I love the drama of it." He sat silently for a moment as if he was waiting for Jake to say something. Finally, he continued. "Okay, you want proof? Here's proof." Derek punched some buttons on the smartphone and pulled up a picture that showed Thomas tied to a chair.

Jake looked at it for a moment and laughed. "Deepfake."

The clone pulled the phone back and swiped across the screen, punched some buttons and held the phone back up for Jake to see. This time a video appeared on screen. It was Thomas, tied to a chair, pleading for Jake's help. After playing the short clip, Derek pulled the phone away.

"Let me talk to him," Jake demanded.

"No," Derek refused. "You've seen enough, now get me into the time machine and I'll tell you where he is."

There was a gentle knock at the door before it opened. Thomas walked in. "Hey bro, got time for lunch?" Realizing that he had interrupted something, he quickly apologized. "Oh, sorry, dude, I didn't know you had somebody in here."

A broad smile crossed Jake's face as he looked at Derek. "It's okay, Thomas. Can you give us a minute?"

"Sure, Bro. I'll wait outside."

Derek's face betrayed the sheer panic he was feeling. He jumped up and tried to push past Jake and get out the door. Jake placed his hand on the clone's chest and shoved him back into the chair.

Derek's sickly copy was significantly lighter and a little smaller than the original. Jake grabbed a pipe wrench that was lying on the table and raised it as though he was going to bludgeon Derek with it. The clone raised his arms over his head and whimpered.

"You're nothing like your predecessor," Jake said. "He put up a lot more fight than you're even capable of. I don't know if you have his memories, but if you do, you'll remember that I was the last person he saw before he died."

The clone peeked around his protective arms and saw that Jake had lowered the pipe wrench. "I only have his memories up to the point that he had me cloned," he said, lowering his arms. "Obviously, that was before you killed him."

"You are a pretty pathetic version of him. I'm at a loss to understand how you managed to kidnap the scientists in the future and hold them against their will."

Derek coughed up some blood. "I was in a little bit better shape then." He said, wiping the blood on his mouth with his shirt. "What are you going to do now?"

"I'm going to let you go. Then I'm going to lunch with my brother, who, as we both know, is not being held captive."

"Why would you let me go?"

"Because I know that if I drag you out of here, you'll start screaming that I'm a mad man and that I'm trying to kill you and it will cause an embarrassing scene that I don't really want to deal with. I would really like to beat you senseless with this pipe wrench, but judging from the shape you're in, you might just drop-dead walking across the parking lot. So, get out of here! Go crawl back to whatever hole you crawled out of and wait. The most brilliant minds on the planet are working on a way to dispose of you in a cleaner, more scientific method. I'm really looking forward to that."

Derek slowly stood up and walked to the door. When he realized that Jake was not going to attack him, he threw the door open and raced out, bumping into Thomas as he hurried away.

"What the heck was that about?" Thomas asked.

"Don't ask," Jake answered. "It's a long story."

"There's something familiar about that guy. Have I met him before?"

"I don't know, maybe. Let's go to lunch."

As Thomas drove to the lunch destination, Jake texted Mia:

Derek is not in the wormhole. He just left my office.

Going to lunch with Thomas. See you soon.

Chapter Twenty

To Catch a Clone

Mia was visibly upset. "I tried calling you after I got your text, but you didn't answer. I've been worried that something happened to you."

"I'm sorry," Jake said, defensively. "I couldn't talk about this on the phone with Thomas right there. He would start asking questions I can't answer. He already asked me who Derek was because he looked familiar."

"Time fragments," Mia said sourly. "Still, you shouldn't try to take him on by yourself. He's dangerous."

Jake laughed. "Not so much anymore," he said with a smile. "It's hard to believe that this is the guy that held you hostage."

"What do you mean?"

"He's a lot smaller than what I remember of the original Derek. And he's sick. He kept coughing, and at one point he spit up blood. He looked older than I remember Derek looking too. When he tried to push past me to get out the door, I shoved him back into his chair. He was a lot lighter than I expected and shoving him like that clearly hurt him. He's not in good shape."

George had been listening to their conversation and asked, "Could that be because he was trapped in a wormhole?"

"I guess it's possible," Mia answered. "Let's bring Henry and Arthur into this conversation."

The two men came up out of the basement and Jake told them about his encounter with Derek.

"Clones don't generally live as long as the originals," Henry said. "And depending on who did the cloning procedures, his DNA could have been damaged. There have been cases in which a fatal disease was accidentally programmed into a clone's DNA. Maybe that's what happened to Derek."

"Do you think being trapped in the wormhole accelerated the aging process?" Mia asked.

"I'm sure it did," Henry said.

"Yes, but we can't just wait around for him to die," Arthur said in his usual dour way. "He could cause a lot of problems before he dies."

"But only if he gets to the time machine, right?" Jake asked.

"Perhaps," George said. "What concerns me is how he got out of the wormhole."

"But he can't get to the machine in the basement, right?" Jake pressed. "You've got some forcefield around it to keep him out, right?"

"The barrier around the house only prevents him from gaining access from a portal, or another time machine," Arthur said. "He could sneak into the house and access it."

"But," Henry interjected, raising his finger to make his point. "If he did, he would be trapped in the microgravity time loop which is exactly where we want him."

"Yes, but what if he has access to another machine, somehow?" George asked again.

"I don't think he does," Jake said. "Why else would he want me to get him to the machine here?"

"That's a valid point to be sure," George said.

"Why don't we just use the locator to find his geographic coordinates and open up a wormhole to pull him back here?" Arthur growled.

"When will you have it working?" Jake asked.

"It's working now," Arthur snapped.

"I thought you just started working on it this morning," Jake said.

"We used the time machine," Arthur grunted.

"Which means, what?" Jake asked.

Mia answered the question. "It took us a week to design and build it. We needed parts and materials that are not available in this time, so we jumped forward to get them. Then we jumped back to today to test it."

"If we would have known that you had a Derek encounter," Arthur growled. "We could have grabbed him then."

"It's no matter," George said. "We can grab him now.

"We can open the wormhole," Henry said, "but somebody is going to have to push him in."

"That's why we have Jake, isn't it?" Arthur questioned.

All eyes were on Jake. It took him a moment to realize what they were volunteering him to do. "Oh, you want me to push him in!"

"Not to worry, Jake," George said. "After dispatching the real Derek, this emaciated clone should be easy work."

"I'm not worried," Jake said confidently. "Let's go get him."

The team was gathered around a sophisticated computer in the basement. In fact, the whole basement had been transformed to a futuristic laboratory. Arthur programmed the clone's DNA into the computer and waited for the results. Soon the computer displayed Derek's GPS coordinates. Jake punched the numbers into the map on his smartphone and a pin showed up at the same location he encountered Derek earlier.

"Looks like he's still at the job site," Jake said. "So, what do we do now? Do I need to go there before you open the portal?"

"That would be best," Mia said. "Once you locate him, we'll open the portal, and you can push him in."

"I'll go with you, Jake," George said. "There's really nothing I can do here."

"How are you going to know when we find him?" Jake asked.

"I've already tapped into some satellite cameras," Arthur said. "We'll be watching. And we have these earpieces you can wear so we can communicate with each other."

George and Jake inserted the earpieces and tested them. Everything seemed to be working. They climbed into Jake's truck and drove to the job site. The sun was just setting when they arrived.

"If we don't hurry," George said, "We're going to need flashlights.

Jake reached behind his seat and grabbed two flashlights. He handed one to George and climbed out of his truck.

"Testing, testing," Jake said. "Can you guys still hear us?"

"Loud and clear," Mia's voice came back through the earpiece.

"Where should we look for him?" George asked.

"I think we'll find him around the back by the scrap pile," Jake suggested.

The two men walked cautiously to the back of the job site. They activated their flashlights and began shining them around, looking for any sign of Derek.

"The clone is about 10 meters to your left," Arthur said.

"There's a big pile of scrap wood over there," Jake answered. "Is he hiding behind it?"

Before anyone could answer a shot rang out. Jake recognized the sound from Thomas' wedding. It was a ray gun from the future. He turned to talk to George, but he was gone. The shot had vaporized him.

Jake immediately ran for cover. "He's got a laser gun," he yelled into his communicator. "He just vaporized George."

Taking cover behind some giant spools of wire, Jake tried to think through the situation. Suddenly, a portal opened up to his right and a small object shot out of it.

"Jake, catch!" Mia's voice rang out in his ears. He reached out and grabbed a futuristic gun like he had at the wedding.

"Now, turn about 10 degrees to your right and fire. Don't think about it. Just fire."

Jake turned slightly to the right and fired the weapon. The heap of wood scraps immediately vanished, exposing the clone.

"You've got to get that gun away from him before we open the portal," Arthur said. "We can't send him into the wormhole with it. No telling what damage he might do."

"I'll just vaporize him and we can figure it out later," Jake yelled as he pulled the trigger. His first shot miraculously hit the clone in the right hand, vaporizing both his hand and the gun. The clone screamed in agony.

"You're clearly not a very good shot," Arthur growled into the communicator.

Jake tried to fire the weapon again, but nothing happened. He threw the gun to the ground.

"Activate the portal," he screamed as he rushed toward the clone. As he neared, he saw that there was no blood coming from Derek's hand. The ray gun must have cauterized it. The portal opened just as

Jake made contact with his adversary. He slammed into Derek with the full weight of his body, sending the smaller man flying backward into the portal. The wormhole immediately closed and the night was suddenly quiet. Jake knelt down, trying to catch his breath. The adrenaline and physical exertion had completely exhausted him.

His thoughts turned to George. He was suddenly filled with anguish. George Holman had fought valiantly to protect the world from potential harm the time machine could cause and lost his life in the process. Who would go back to 1920 and tell his family? How could they possibly tell his wife what happened? Did she even know about the time machine?

"George is gone," he panted into his communicator.

"We know," Arthur said, bluntly.

"Jake," Mia said calmly. "Come back to the house."

Jake walked to his truck and drove back home. He felt responsible for George's death. He dreaded facing his wife and the other scientists who had worked so closely with George. He pulled up in front of the house and turned off the engine. He sat in the driver's seat thinking about the confrontation with Derek. He remembered that young Zander had used the time machine to save older Zander after he was shot at Thomas' wedding. With sudden optimism, he bolted from his truck and ran up the walkway to the front door. He burst through the door only to run headlong into George, sending both men tumbling to the floor.

"Whoa there, cowboy," George chuckled, "Take it easy."

"George!" Jake exclaimed. "Did they already go back in time to save you?" "No," George replied with a grin. "We can't use the machine until we're finished with the clone."

"Then how are you here? You were vaporized."

"Dear boy," George said with a smile. "Derek is not the only person who can make a clone."

Chapter Twenty-One

The End of an Era

Jake awoke to the sound of a crying baby. He was alone in bed. Mia had already gotten up to take care of the infant. He went downstairs to see if he could help. Mia was trying to make a bottle with one hand while holding the baby with her other arm.

"Here, let me make that for you," Jake said as he took the bottle and filled it with formula. Mia took the bottle and rubbed the nipple on the baby's lips, prompting her to latch on and start feeding. The new parents sat together on the couch while Mia fed the baby.

Fourteen months had passed since they captured Derek's clone in the wormhole. George Holman stayed with them until they brought the clone's remains out. Jake never knew what they did with him after that, and he didn't want to ask. George eventually returned to the past. Arthur and Henry traveled to the future.

Mia gave birth to a baby girl, who they named, Janet, in honor of Thomas' first wife. The new parents were still adjusting to having a baby in the house. Jake took some time off work to help Mia around the house.

The time machine had remained unused in the basement and Jake hoped it would stay that way. But he knew that it wouldn't. He worried that Mia would get homesick for the future she grew up in and want to go back. He also wondered about the consequences of marrying and having a baby with a woman who was hundreds of years younger than him.

"Jake," Mia said, interrupting his thoughts. "There's something I've been meaning to tell you."

"Uh oh," Jake said apprehensively. "What is it?"

"Henry is our descendent."

"What? How do you know?"

"His parent's named him after the ancestor who built this house, so his family knew his lineage. When he showed me his family tree, I noticed that someone named Jake, who's wife's name was Mia, were in his ancestral line. At first, I thought it was an interesting coincidence. But when George staged me in your time to watch for Derek, I knew that I was going to marry you. When I first got here, though, you were in the Army. It wasn't until you were discharged that I got to meet you. For me, it was love at first sight."

"It was for me too," Jake said.

The couple sat in silence for a few minutes and Jake started drifting off to sleep. Mia gently nudged him. "Why don't you go back to bed."

Jake trudged up the stairs, flopped into bed and was asleep in seconds. The baby finished her bottle and fell asleep. Mia put her back in her crib and crawled back in bed.

The next morning, when Jake awoke, Mia was already dressed and ready for the day. He dragged himself out of bed, took a shower and dressed.

As usual, Mia had breakfast ready when he got downstairs. As they sat eating breakfast, the doorbell rang. Jake got up to answer it. He opened the door to find an elderly man standing on his front porch.

"Can I help you?" Jake asked.

"Don't you recognize me, Jake?" What was recognizable was the distinct British accent. It belonged to George Holman, but he was considerably older than the last time Jake saw him. "George?" he asked.

"In the flesh," George answered. "May I come in?"

"Of course. Why didn't you come up through the basement?"

"I thought perhaps I should use the front door for once, since now, it is your home."

"Did you come here in the time machine?"

"Of course, I did. But I used the tunnel to the outside and came around to the front door."

George followed Jake into the kitchen. Mia looked up to see who was with him and did a double take.

"George?" she asked, peering at him through narrow eyes.

"Yes, it's me," George answered. "Just a tad older than the last time you saw me."

"You're a lot more than a tad older," Jake laughed.

"Which is why I've come today," George said. "As you can see, I've gotten older and I'm afraid this might be the last time we see each other."

"We've got a time machine," Mia protested. "We can come back and see you when you're younger any time we want."

"Yes, I know," George said. "But for me in my timeline, I know that my remaining time is short. My wife has already passed on. She succumbed to cancer several years ago. My children are all grown and gone and I'm alone in the house."

"I'm sorry to hear about your wife," Mia said.

"So am I," Jake said.

"And you're welcome here anytime." Mia said. "You can even come here to live if you want."

"Thank you," George said. "I appreciate the offer, but my children are close by, and they look in on me frequently. I just wanted to let you know that since the last time we met - which for me was quite a few years ago – there hasn't been any activity in the time machine that I'm aware of. It appears that we have succeeded in securing the timeline."

"Have you heard anything from Arthur or Henry?" Mia asked.

"Not a word," George answered.

"We haven't either," Mia said. "But it's only been a little over a year for us."

"Much longer for me," George winked. He looked at Jake and Mia for a moment before continuing. "Anyway, it's been a pleasure working with you both and I'm so glad you've found happiness together."

"Mia had a baby girl," Jake blurted.

"Really?" George asked. "May I see her?"

Mia brought Janet out and placed her in George's arms.

"She's beautiful," George said after looking at her for a moment.

"One of the truly incredible things about time traveling for me has been the opportunity I've had to meet some of my descendants that one normally wouldn't meet in one's lifetime. Not many people get to do that."

He handed the baby back to Mia. "I don't mean to take up your time, I just wanted to say goodbye and thank you for the incredible experiences I've been a part of. And if you ever see Arthur and Henry again, give them my regards."

George turned toward to the front door to make his exit, but Jake intercepted him. "You don't need to use the front door. You built this house. Let us go down to the basement with you to see you off."

George descended the stairs followed by Jake and Mia who was carrying the baby. George walked across the floor and opened the bookcase that hid the stairs to the room that housed the time machine. Before he descended the stairs, he turned back to Jake and Mia. He hugged them both.

"We're going to miss you George," Jake said as tears welled up in his eyes.

"Yes, we will," Mia agreed.

"As will I," George said. "It's truly been my honor." With that he walked down the stairs to the time machine.

Jake and Mia stood in the basement as the turbines wound up to speed with the familiar sound. After a few minutes the humming sound ceased, and George had returned to his time in the past.

The couple solemnly climbed the stairs. Jake walked into the living room and threw himself onto the couch.

"Aren't you going to work today?" Mia asked.

"No, I think I'll take the day off," Jake said glumly. "I'm not in the mood for work today."

"I understand, honey. I'm going to miss him too."

"Do you think we should destroy the time machine?" Jake asked.

"No," Mia protested. "We have to preserve it to safeguard the space-time continuum."

"Yeah, I know. George gave me specific instructions to watch for time travelers."

"How are you going to know if you find any?" Mia asked.

"That's a good question. *You* certainly had me fooled."

"I'm glad you know the truth now and that it didn't freak you out."

"Something just occurred to me," Jake said. "When you lived in the future, and you already knew that you would travel back to the past and marry me. Did you already have memories of our life together?"

Mia smiled. "Some questions are better left unanswered," she said coyly.

Jake mulled her answer over for a moment. "So, you *do* know what's going to happen in our lives together."

"Honey, we have a time machine in our basement. We can see the future together, or we can just live it one day at a time."

About the Author

Dan Curtis is a musician, composer, audiobook narrator and author. Dan has written and produced several children's e-books, narrated by his daughter, Cheyenne. Over the course of his music career, he has produced several dozen advertising jingles, two personalized children's music albums as well as solo music albums. He is currently working on a children's music album with his daughter, Cheyenne.

Currently, he has three audiobooks from classic literature that he narrated and published:

- The Legend of Sleepy Hollow
- The Monkey's Paw
- A Christmas Carol

The audiobooks have sound effects and music to enhance the dramatic effect of the narration.

In addition to these audiobooks, Dan produced a comedic audiobook called, The Adventures of Munson and Murph that follows the escapes of two completely inept investigators. Dan voices more than 25 characters in the program.

Visit him online at https://dancurtismusic.com

Dan lives in Arizona with his wife and children.